The
PATH
of the
JAGUAR

ALSO BY STEPHEN HENIGHAN

NOVELS

Other Americas
The Places Where Names Vanish
The Streets of Winter

SHORT STORY COLLECTIONS

Nights in the Yungas
North of Tourism
A Grave in the Air

NON-FICTION

Assuming the Light: The Parisian Literary Apprenticeship of
    Miguel Ángel Asturias
When Words Deny the World: The Reshaping of Canadian Writing
Lost Province: Adventures in a Moldovan Family
A Report on the Afterlife of Culture
A Green Reef: The Impact of Climate Change
Sandino's Nation: Ernesto Cardenal and Sergio Ramírez Writing
    Nicaragua, 1940-2012

The
PATH
of the
JAGUAR

STEPHEN HENIGHAN

thistledown press

Thistledown Press Ltd.
410 2nd Avenue North
Saskatoon, Saskatchewan, S7K 2C3
www.thistledownpress.com

Library and Archives Canada Cataloguing in Publication

Henighan, Stephen, 1960 –, author
The path of the jaguar / Stephen Henighan.

Issued in print and electronic formats.
ISBN 978-1-77187-123-5 (paperback).– ISBN 978-1-77187-125-9 (html).– ISBN 978-1-77187-124-2 (pdf)
I. Title.
PS8565.E5818P38 2016   C813'.54   C2016-905260-5
C2016-905261-3

Cover and book design by Jackie Forrie
Printed and bound in Canada

Canada Council   Conseil des Arts
for the Arts   du Canada

SASKATCHEWAN
ARTS BOARD

Canadä

Thistledown Press gratefully acknowledges the financial assistance of the Canada Council for the Arts, the Saskatchewan Arts Board, and the Government of Canada for its publishing program.

The
PATH
of the
JAGUAR

PART ONE

1997

ONE

"AND YOUR CHILD?" MAMA SAID from the doorway. Thinking of the child in her belly, not the girl playing in front of the television, Amparo avoided her mother's eyes. She looked at her leather shoes and straightened her white blouse over the hips of her black dress slacks. When a woman's husband makes false accusations, she can share her pain with no one. The sickness of the silence between her and Eusebio, as acrid as morning sickness except that it was continuing into her fifth month, filled her throat. Stepping out of the doorway into the shadow of the room's zinc roof, her mother said: "Do you want me to look after Sandra while you go to town?"

"Inés can look after her. She can close the stall for a few hours."

"Let her keep working. I'll look after your daughter." Her mother bent forward and hugged Sandra to the yellow stitching that crossed her light blue *huipil*: the same blouse that Amparo wore when she sold handicrafts in the market, but which she exchanged for Western clothes when she left the village. "Don't you want to help your nana husk black beans?"

As Sandra squealed, Amparo yearned to be able to fall into her mother's arms. "Speak to her in Cakchiquel, Mama. Teach her our language better than you taught it to us."

Amparo's mother hugged her granddaughter to her chest. "When I was young we were dirty Indians until we spoke Spanish, and then maybe we could be people."

"I'm going, Mama." She pulled her jacket around her shoulders, zipping it up so that her belly would not shock the nuns. As they crossed the tiles to the front door, Amparo caught herself saying goodbye to Sandra in Spanish. She was like her mother: she wanted her daughter to speak Spanish. She told herself that if her mother had passed on her entire culture, she would have been spared this embarrassment.

She opened the gate of the compound and stepped onto the dirt street where bougainvillea spilled over the tops of the white stucco walls. The steep slopes of the valley climbed towards the sunlight. The brightness hurt her eyes; when she and Eusebio were first married, they used to meet in Antigua at the end of the day and ride the bus home together up the mountainside

She turned left towards the village's small concrete park. It had no trees or fountain like the park in Antigua. Averting her eyes from the house on the corner with the purple door, she entered the market. A new stucco building, put up next to the town hall by a Swedish aid project as the Peace Accords were being signed, it was dim and spacious, lined by the women's ceiling-high stalls draped with weaving. Most of the wall-hangings, bags and vests were woven at home by women and girls on backstrap looms or smaller *telas de cincha*; some of the work was mass-produced, with synthetics blended into the wool. The mayor had raised the licence fee for stalls again, and the women were taking home fewer quetzales. Coming from a family that had enough food to support a servant, Amparo could send Inés to look after her stall while she cared for Sandra or worked in Antigua. On weekends, when tour buses arrived, she tended the stall herself. She got to know the drivers and

10

guides from the agencies in Antigua, acquaintanceships that led to special commissions or private sales.

Amparo entered the market, greeting the women in Cakchiquel mixed with Spanish. A thin hand caught her arm. The girl held a baby at her breast. As a child, she had been the terror of the market. In school her learning was so quick that she took over the class on days when the teacher was drunk. There was talk of a scholarship that would allow her to go to secondary school with the nuns in Antigua. But in early adolescence, those dangerous months for a young girl, when she had finished the six years of primary schooling and was waiting to find out whether she could study with the nuns, she had fallen in love. By her fourteenth birthday she was pregnant; now married, she would never leave the market. Watching the baby's curled hands pat the girl's cheek, Amparo wished Mama were stricter with Yolanda. On the day Sandra was born, as soon as the midwife told her she had a girl, Amparo promised herself that her daughter would not take a walk with a boy until she had finished secondary school.

"Doña Amparo," the girl said. "My mother and I want to join your savings club."

"Ask your mother to talk to me."

"She's gone to get the bus to Antigua."

"I'll see her on the bus then. I'm going to Antigua myself." She made her way to her stall in the back corner of the market. Weavings made by Inés, by Amparo's mother, by her sisters and sisters-in-law and by Amparo herself, stretched down from racks and hangers in the dim light. She reached down, slipping her hand into a pile of stacked blankets, and pulled out the dark red bag. B'alam. Once a year, sometimes more often, she wove a red bag with an ambling white jaguar on the side. When she was tending the stall she hung the bag above her head. Don

11

Julio had tried to arrange for her to go to Mexico — to Chiapas and Oaxaca — to meet indigenous women, exchange weaving techniques and sell her bags. She had dreamed that this could come true, as though she were a rich *käk winaq* with a passport, as though Mexico would give her a visa. In the end, Don Julio had shipped the bags to Mexico; Amparo stayed at home.

"How's it going?" Inés looked startled at Amparo's question. The vertical pleats of her grey-blue Quiché skirt lent her hips a fragile air. Her eyes met Amparo's, then skidded away, still afraid of her after all these years. During the civil war the girl's village in the highlands was occupied by the army: the soldiers raped every Mayan girl as soon as she reached puberty. Amparo's father made deliveries in the region and sometimes spent the night in the home of Inés' parents. When the child turned eight, her father asked Papa to take her away. "But you haven't met my wife," Papa said. "You don't know what sort of woman your daughter will be working for." He feared that Inés would simply add to his family's burdens. That night, he told Amparo, he drove his truck back to Guatemala City, keeping himself awake by swigging his favourite cocktail of black coffee and Coca-Cola from his thermos. Inés slept on the seat beside him, her sandals grazing the top of the woven bag on the floor that held her clothes. He delivered his load of wood hewn from a highland forest to a furniture factory on the edge of the capital, then brought the girl back to the village. The next time Amparo's father drove north, the army had razed the girl's village. The place no longer existed; to ask what had happened to the people who lived there was to invite death. When he told the girl, she lowered her head. She stopped asking when she would go home. After Amparo and Eusebio married, her father gave them Inés as a wedding present.

"I sold a bag to a gringo couple," Inés said. Her meek smile reminded Amparo that she was twenty. She should have married by now; her humble manner suggested that she would not marry, that she would always be a burden.

Inés showed her the money paid by the gringos. Amparo counted it and slid it into the pocket of her dress slacks. "I'm going to Antigua," Amparo said. "You close the stall when you finish."

"*Sí, señora,*" Inés said. They spoke in Spanish, even though Cakchiquel and the girl's Quiché shared many words.

Amparo left the market and walked across the whitewashed park and up the street of interlocking stone to where the bus to Antigua waited.

Ten passengers sat on the yellow-and-black schoolbus, its front window plastered with decals announcing the driver's personal relationship with Jesus Christ. The *pilotos* of public buses were converts to Evangelical Protestantism. Papa was a *piloto*, even if he drove trucks rather than buses, and he remained an observant Catholic. She felt more secure when her driver was a God-fearing Catholic rather than an upstart Evangelical so arrogant as to mistake God's son for his personal friend.

"Amparo, come here, *mi hija*," Doña María called.

In her slurred Spanish, Doña María asked about Amparo's mother's health. They might have understood each other better in Cakchiquel, but Doña María was embarrassed to use the language in public. She had been unable to go to the market in Antigua this morning because her youngest was ill. She was making the trip down the mountainside with a bag of potatoes, even though it was late in the day and the chances of selling enough to cover the bus fare were slender.

"I would like to save my money."

13

"I saw your daughter in the market," Amparo said. "How pretty her baby looks."

"You must be looking forward to your next baby, *mi hija*. Is your husband hoping for a son?"

Amparo felt the fullness of her stomach as though the child were heating her. Her temples throbbed. Papa claimed that Doña María had the powers of a *curandera*, like her sister Eduviges. The driver kicked the bus into gear and made a tour of the block, the *ayudante* hanging out the open door by his arm and yelling, "Antigua! Antigua!" as he scanned the streets for passengers. She braced her hand against the back of the seat in front of her above where the mysterious word "*Bluebird*" was pressed into the dark green metal. The bus began to climb out of the valley.

Doña María, rocking alongside her, said: "Your child will not go hungry. The women in your savings club are rich."

"We're not rich, Doña María. We are humble people who are saving our money."

"The government and the gringos gave you money and you're keeping it for yourselves." Doña María's face underwent a hideous transformation. "Why won't you let me join?"

"Our club," Amparo said, "was set up by a Non-Governmental Organization. Every woman must deposit six quetzales a month. At the end of the year, if we've followed the law, the bank pays us our interest and the government matches a portion of our savings with a donation — "

"The government gives you money and doesn't give any to the rest of us! That's your payoff for telling the women in the market to vote for President Arzú."

"No, that's not how it works. We are audited by the government, we are overseen by a gringa development worker. If we are not moral, if we are not meticulous — "

14

"*Eleq'om ri ixoq!* The woman's a thief!" Doña María switched into Cakchiquel. "Everybody knows that you and your friends meet in the basement of your church to count your money!"

"It's not very much money," Amparo said, wishing she could avoid this part of the conversation. She spoke in Cakchiquel, hoping that the lounging teenage boys in baseball caps at the back of the bus would ignore them. "In the future we will be able to take out the money as *micro-crédito*, to start a business or make an investment, but the señora gringa must approve the project, strict records are kept . . . "

"Why can't I join your club?"

"All indigenous women in the village are eligible." The language of bureaucracy edged the conversation back into Spanish.

"*Bueno,*" Doña María said, as though the matter were resolved. "I'm joining. So is my daughter."

The bus clattered around a corner and stopped. Two women and five children climbed on and stood in the aisle. The *ayudante* swung back through the crowd to collect their fares.

"To be a member," Amparo said, "you must send your children to school."

"My daughter was the best student in her year."

"But your sons — "

"My husband needs our sons to work in the *milpa*. It's easy for you: your family has a compound. We must grow corn!"

"You know the conditions, Doña María." Amparo couldn't help admiring the fact that Doña María sent her daughters to school. In many families the girls never saw a classroom; it was the boys who went to school until they grew big enough to help their fathers in the cornfields.

The bus stopped at the bend in the road and a group of children on their way home from school spilled out the door. A seat near the front became free. Dragging her sack of potatoes, Doña María changed seats.

Amparo slid over to the window. Below her lay Antigua. She could see the turmoil of the market beneath the volcanoes, the firm bar of the divided Calzada, packed with trucks and buses, ruling off the market from the town. The spires of the enormous ruined white churches stretched up from the geometrical rectangle of cobblestoned streets that lay like an elongated grate reaching from the Calzada to the park, green with trees, bright with the sprinkle of its invisible fountain and penned in by the heavy buildings that had been built by Spanish Conquistadors. On the north side of the park stood the Cathedral, where God's grace called out to her. North of the park the ruined churches alternated with green interior gardens hidden from the street by white stucco walls and high wooden gates. The enclosed mansions converted into gringo hotels, heavily guarded shops selling jade jewellery, paintings or handicrafts, extended in straight cobblestoned lines to the top of the town. In the moment before the schoolbus dived down the slope, whisking the perfect view from sight, Amparo thought: I don't need to do anything in my life. I don't need to make money or work, or even be happy with my husband because God has made so much beauty for me. Look at all that my God has made for me! I could devote my whole life to thanking God for sending his son Jesus Christ to earth, to thanking Ixmucane for making it possible for women to have children.

As the bus swayed down the potholed dirt streets on the edge of Antigua, the whining of Laura Pausini, singing laments in Spanish about men leaving women, sliced by the sibilant "s"s of her Italian accent, yielded to the voice of a newsreader. They rumbled into the market, rolling over the ruts alongside schoolbuses arriving from other villages. The perfect cone of the Agua Volcano stretched towards the sky. " . . . *the body of the Mayan priest Jorge Puuc has been discovered in a well. Edmundo Rodríguez, known as Comandante Vladimir, spokesman for the guerrillas during the peace negotiations, denounced Puuc's death as evidence that human rights abuses are continuing in spite of the signing of the Peace Accords . . .* " The bus stopped and people filed off into the back quarter of the market, where the furniture makers had their stalls.

Amparo ducked beneath the speaker and eased herself down into the din of the market. Comandante Vladimir was the first guerrilla she had seen on television. For years they had been told that the guerrillas were Soviet ogres, and suddenly there was this handsome man with his gallant moustache and diction more refined than that of any general, representing the guerrillas at the negotiating table. Her friend Raquel, who hated the guerrillas, claimed that Vladimir was as corrupt as the generals.

At her feet, tethered brown chickens clucked their avail-ability for slaughter, pyramids of sapodilla fruit, mandarins, guavas, and mangoes rose from tarpaulins like miniature volcanic cones. She skirted the indoor portion of the market, where food was sold, making her way in the direction of the Calzada. Men stood behind public weigh scales and tables holding telephones. Every vendor barked out the worth of his merchandise: T-shirts, vinyl bags adorned with comic-strip characters, plastic sandals, running shoes. Amparo negotiated the space between the stalls and the streaming people with dazed hesitation. Her balance felt wrong. Her foot slipped on a rut. She caught herself. She must care for her child. *Ri aköla*, she corrected. Not child: children. The second one was already part of her life.

She turned the corner into the alley leading out to the Calzada. Laura Pausini's whine yielded to the manly drama of

Ricardo Arjona. Coming down the alley, Amparo spotted her sister Esperanza hurrying in the direction of the bus back to the village. They exchanged a soft, *"La utz a'wech?"* — "How's it going?" This was as much Cakchiquel as Amparo spoke in Antigua. Four men from a village farther up the mountainside walked past. The two older men wore Mayan garb; the young men were dressed in bluejeans and T-shirts with English words written on them. Amparo crossed the two lanes of slow traffic on the Calzada and entered the calm cobblestoned streets of Antigua.

It took her only five minutes to make her way to the Escuela San Fernando. She climbed the broad stone steps, laid in the sixteenth century, that had remained unbudged by all the earthquakes that had rocked the city. Hot sunlight fell on her face. She went through the swinging front door. A pale-skinned nun stood in the corridor, the cries of children echoing behind her. "May I help you?" she said, her voice revealing that she was from Spain.

"Buenas tardes. My name is Amparo Ajuix. I've come about the job . . . "

"Buenas tardes. I am Sister Consuelo. Please come this way."

As she followed the straight-backed nun down the corridor, Amparo thought: a married woman who talks to others about her husband betrays the sanctity of matrimony. But to confide in a nun . . . that would be like talking to God, like consulting one's own conscience.

Sister Consuelo opened the door and admitted Amparo to a small, spare office with a crucifix on the wall. Amparo sat down, wondering what the nun would ask her. As she struggled to remember the answers she had prepared, the thought struck her that confiding in a nun would be no betrayal at all.

TWO

"YOU'LL HAVE TO WORK LONGER hours in the market," Amparo told Inés over dinner, "because I have a job." She straightened Sandra on her lap. "*¡Frijolitos!*"

Laying down her fork, the girl went to the stove. She brought the scuffed tin pot from the dim alcove and scraped the hot black bean paste onto Amparo's plate.

"My wife plans to spend even more time away from home," Eusebio said from the head of the table. "Our daughter will be brought up by strangers."

"My mother and my sisters will look after Sandra," Amparo said, spooning *frijoles* into Sandra's mouth. "That's our custom."

Eusebio straightened up. She had undercut his social advantage: the fact that, although his skin was as dark as hers, he was not an Indian. He had grown up in a poor neighbourhood on the edge of Antigua, two generations removed from his last relative who had spoken an indigenous language, a fact which elevated him to the status of *ladino*, a person of European culture.

"Yes, it's your custom that all sorts of things are shared." Eusebio got to his feet.

In spite of herself, Amparo stared at him. This was as close as he had come to repeating before others the words he had spoken in their bedroom. He crossed the room. Once she had seen an easygoing tolerance in his slow gait. Sandra moaned

19

and pushed away the next spoonful of *frijoles*. Amparo realized that she was holding her daughter too tightly. Eusebio snapped on the television and sat down on the sofa with his back to the table.

"Inés, please take Sandra to Eusebio. Let him look after her while you and I wash the dishes."

The girl got up, picked up Sandra in her thin arms, and carried her across the room. Amparo felt her muscles tightening. She concentrated on the image of the Baby Jesus, on Xpiyacoc and Ixmucane making the first people out of corn, the first four men who all took the name *B'alam*, Jaguar. Behind her Eusebio was absorbed in a *telenovela* they used to watch together, holding Sandra between them.

In the alcove, soaping the pots for the girl to scrub in the steel sink, Amparo said: "I'm going to be a teacher. I'll teach with the nuns." She handed her the frying pan. "When I started school my poor father worked in the *milpa*. He had nothing to sell but his corn and no money to buy us shoes. The humiliation! Walking into school in bare feet! I begged my mother to let me stay home — "

The volume of the television rose as a pair of illicit lovers exchanged rapturous whispers in Venezuelan accents. Eusebio had always listened to her memories of her family's rise from poverty. Each telling had been different, each version probing a distinct moment of change, examining an emotion she had not considered before. Eusebio, the shy, round-faced *ladino* who approached life with more tranquillity and less striving than she, had made her experiences real.

"And . . . ?" Inés said, as though expecting her to continue.

"Finish the washing," Amparo said.

Her daughter was asleep in her husband's arms. Inés finished the washing up, then retreated through the door leading to the adjoining shed that Amparo's brothers had renovated into a servant's room. Amparo looked past her husband. Their bedroom, its double doors closed, lay behind the television; the room their daughter would share with her brother or sister was next door. Amparo crossed the cool tiles until she stood behind Eusebio. She lifted Sandra off his shoulders. He gave a start. His eyes reproached her for a second. He watched the television.

Sandra, waking, began to sob. "You don't want to be with Mama?" Amparo murmured. "Come with me, *mi vida*, your Mama loves you."

She put her daughter to bed, sensing the little girl's apprehension at the brisk movements with which she undressed her. As Amparo turned to leave the bedroom, Sandra said: "I'm afraid, Mama. Don't turn out the light."

Amparo sat down on the bed. "I'll tell you a story," she said. "My grandmother told me this story when I was a little girl. To tell this story right, you must tell it in Cakchiquel. You can't tell it in Spanish because it is the story of how the Spanish people took our ancestors' land."

"When did they do that?"

"In the 16th century. But of course our ancestors did not call that time the 16th century. They used a different calendar."

"What did our ancestors call that time?"

"I don't know, Sandra. I'm very sorry. I don't know the Mayan calendar well enough . . . " She paused. "I will tell you the story." She wondered whether she would be able to get through the formal Cakchiquel of the oral storyteller without making a mistake. As she prepared to speak, she realized that the television had been turned off. The house was silent. The ceiling light in the main room had been extinguished; only the lamp next to the sofa was on. Eusebio was listening.

21

Sliding across the bed to hold Sandra in her arms, she said: "*Pa ri q'ij Jun Junajpu', xe'oqa ri Xexa' Winäq pa taq qulew. Ri q'iy re' xtikir k'a ri kamisanik, ri eläq, ri meb'a'il chi qakojol. Pa ri q'ij re' chuqa xeyakatäj ri qati't qaMama' richin ma nki'ya ta ki' chi kiwäch re winäq re'. Chi koköj chi nima'q xkichäp k'a ri oyowal xeb'e pa taq q'ayis richin nikiya ruchoq'a ri lab'al . . .*"

She pronounced the words with care, reviewing their meaning in her mind: One day, says the writer, the foreigners, the *ladinos*, came to our land. That day the massacre began, the theft, there were little orphans among us. On that day also our ancestors rose up, they did not let themselves disappear, they confronted those people. Young and old were seized by rage, by anger. They went off to the mountains. They left behind the products of their work, their woven clothes.

She did not translate her words aloud. Sandra would have to work out the Cakchiquel for herself. Amparo kissed her daughter good night and turned out the light. She walked past Eusebio and into their bedroom. It was so late when he came to bed that she was barely conscious of his weight on the mattress. She curled around her belly until sleep claimed her.

THREE

SISTER CONSUELO WATCHED HER TEACH the girls, standing next to the green blackboard at the edge of the courtyard. Amparo finished the lesson by leading the children through the alphabet. As the little girls in their checkered skirts and white blouses walked to the door, the young nun came over and took Amparo's arm.

Crossing the courtyard beneath the bright sunlight, Amparo heard the echoes return: the silenced voices of those who had died when the Spaniards came, the voices of the first nuns who had prayed here in Latin more than four centuries ago, the grumbling of the earthquake that had emptied the city two centuries later. She felt history rise like an adobe wall between her and the Spanish nun at the same time that she was touched by the nun's gentleness, her freedom from prejudice. "I think you will be a good teacher, Amparo. One can see that you are accustomed to talking to children."

"In Guatemala we're surrounded by children."

"Most of those children don't study. Yet you, who are from a village, have a good education. How did that happen?" Sister Consuelo indicated a bench. They sat down.

"I always wanted to learn. I didn't want to get married until I had become a real person. When I was a little girl I hated school . . . so many children and the teacher absent or drunk . . . I will never send my children to a state school! No matter how poor I am, I will pay for them to come to a school like this one. "

She glanced over; the nun's expectant face bid her to continue. "When I finished the six years of school my father had stopped growing corn and got a job as a truck driver. He never drank; he saved his salary. He bought the plot of land next to our house, then the plot next to that one. We all worked. I went to a trade school for girls to learn sewing and more writing and arithmetic, then I went into a Korean *maquila* in the capital and sewed shirts. Hours of sewing every day without being allowed to talk to the girl next to me. I felt like I was dead. I was coughing all the time, I'd almost forgotten how to think."

"Did you pray to Our Lord for his counsel?"

"Always, sister. I saved money to help my parents because my father was fencing in the land he had bought and building a compound for the family, with five small houses inside the compound. I worked in the *maquila* for two years. After the first year, I started taking night classes towards my secondary diploma, but I kept missing them and falling asleep because I was so tired. Finally my father said: 'If you are serious about doing this, take the time and do it.'"

Sister Consuelo looked away, staring in the direction of the old Tzutujil groundskeeper who was sweeping the far corner of the yard with a reed broom. "You owe a great deal to your parents."

Amparo nodded. "When I signed up in at the Escuela Díaz de Castillo in Antigua, my father paid. I left the *maquila* and got a job in El Tesoro waiting on tables." She assumed that she did not need to mention Don Julio. "I did school work all night. I finished when I was twenty. I was the first person in my family to receive a secondary school diploma. My sister and one of my brothers have followed me. Three of us, out of ten children.

Few families have so many high-school graduates. My youngest sister, Yolanda, could be the fourth. But she's seventeen and is too sociable . . . How I hope she doesn't fall in love!" Noticing Sister Consuelo's troubled gaze, she said: "In Guatemala it is very dangerous for a girl to fall in love."

"Human love is always ephemeral," Sister Consuelo said. "The only love of which we may be certain is that of the Lord." She looked away from the building that combined school and convent. Amparo watched the nun take in, as if for the first time, the shape of her body. "After the love of the Lord, the next best is the love of a mother for her child because it is selfless and because it is a tribute to the Virgin's love for the divine infant. You wish to have many children?"

"Yes, sister." Amparo looked at her black leather shoes, scuffed by the dust of the courtyard. She did not dare tell Sister Consuelo that in spite of the firmness of her faith, in this detail she could not follow the church's mandates. Mama had given birth twelve times. Yolanda, born when Mama was forty-three, had almost killed her. Mama never would have had this last child if not for Papa's belief that a man loses respect unless his wife gives birth every year. Amparo had been ten. She remembered Mama's groans, the doctor rushing in to help the midwife, the door slamming shut behind them while she stood outside holding her sister and her brother. They waited all night for the news that they had lost their mother. In the morning she was alive and the gasping child who would grow up to be a disobedient girl had joined them. A week later, when her mother emerged from the bedroom, her face was strained and she walked with a stiff, rollicking gait, her spine wrenched out of shape by this final ordeal of labour. Amparo, knowing she could not escape marriage and might one day even desire it, promised herself that she would have no more than two children. "But I also wish to work. I wish to progress." She halted, afraid she might have offended the nun. "Not to progress in the world — I only want enough money to support my family — but to do work that is not boring, to help people and to develop as a person."

"We must be content with the work God allots us, Amparo."

"Yes, sister." Amparo looked at the green-painted slats of the bench.

After leaving work, she walked down the broad steps of the Escuela San Fernando and turned into the cobblestoned street. Glimmering white cloud had smeared the summit of the Agua Volcano. Beneath the cloud, the cone's upper slopes had been drenched a darker shade of green. Amparo distinguished the miniature coils of grey unfurling from distant fires. The feeling of connection to a landscape that was halfway to God mingled heaven and earth before her eyes.

Schoolchildren streamed past in their uniforms, buffeting tourists unaccustomed to walking on rounded stones. The thought of an evening at home made her mouth taste bad. She turned in the direction of the park.

The old Chinese man had retired since her last walk through the centre: his hardware store had become a hotel; there were two new cafés owned by gringos. The girls serving in the cafés had good educations and spoke a little English. Amparo would make sure that Sandra learned English; the truth was, she wanted to learn it herself. She feared that if she expressed her desire to Sister Consuelo, the nun would condemn her worldliness. Don Julio had grasped her hunger to understand. That was why, even though they had barely spoken since she had disappointed him, she must go to see him.

FOUR

THE FOUNTAIN IN THE PARK reminded her of the days when she had been Don Julio's brightest hope. The blond backpackers sat on benches among the low shrubs and the women in their dark blue *huipiles* — Cakchiqueles, too, but from Lake Atitlán — unfolded woven goods for the gringos' admiration and sold them at inflated prices while the ice cream vendors pushed carts over the cobbles and rang their bells. She had barely walked through the park since the beginning of her pregnancy. Glimpsing the white façade of the Cathedral through the eucalyptus trees, she paused for an instant's reminder of peace and forgiveness before she turned towards El Tesoro.

Located half a block off the park, El Tesoro specialized in selling pancake breakfasts with enormous side dishes of sliced fruit, dark local coffee and mango or papaya *licuados* to tourists who sat at tables of varnished wood in the shadow of the covered interior courtyard. Next to the restaurant was a handicraft store selling local coffee in small, expensive bags, woven goods of indifferent quality, as well as postcards and guide books in English, Spanish, French, German, and Italian. The front room of El Tesoro was a bookstore. Many of the books were in English. After she had completed her secondary school diploma, Don Julio had suggested that she move from waiting on tables to working in the bookstore. Amparo felt a gulf of uneasy wonder. She, the daughter of a woman who could barely read, working in a bookstore! And one where many of the books were in English. They were not, Don Julio explained, the sort of books read by tourists. The bulk of his stock was about Guatemala. Amparo marvelled at the discovery that gringos had spent years studying the civil war or religion or land use, or, to her astonishment, the history, archeology, language, and traditions of Mayan people. She leafed through the pages, recognizing the word "Maya" and an occasional place name or photograph. A feeling of rage and triumph surged up in her. If foreigners who wrote books in English found the Maya worthy of meticulous appreciation, who were the *ladinos* to despise indigenous people? She had always been active in her community, in the market and in women's groups affiliated with the Catholic Church. After Don Julio moved her to the bookstore, she had worked even harder to promote her culture.

"But Don Julio, I don't speak English." She was terrified of jeopardizing this opportunity, but she respected him too much not to be honest.

Don Julio gave a quick nod from behind his steel-rimmed glasses. His manner was commanding but not arrogant; his years in exile had softened his *ladino* presumption. A student in the 1960s, Don Julio had fled the country at the beginning of the civil war. He had completed his studies in Mexico City; he lived there for years. In 1990, when the fighting had contracted to remote areas of the highlands and intellectuals had ceased to disappear in the night, he returned to Guatemala. An uncle had left him part of the income of a coffee plantation. Don Julio used the money to buy El Tesoro. The restaurant and the handicraft store made the business profitable, he confided, but the bookstore was his treasure. That was why he had located it at the front of the building: visitors must walk past the books to reach their food or souvenirs. "You do not need to speak English," he said in a soft voice. "The clients who are interested in these books are professors and students. They speak Spanish. They will be pleased that the woman serving them is herself Maya." She spied a flash of cunning in the flex of his silver brows. As much as a compliment to her abilities, the offer was a strategy to give Don Julio's business the face he wished it to have in the country that was coming to be as the civil war receded. Her rueful exasperation yielded before the hopeful thought that if Don Julio was promoting the integration of Mayan people into postwar society — they all knew the war must end, even though at that point it was not over — others might do the same.

"You will also find," Don Julio pointed to the shelves that stood against the wall, "that it is the foreigners, not our own ignorant *burguesía*, who are interested in Guatemalan literature."

She had read books by Miguel Ángel Asturias and Luis Cardoza y Aragón in secondary school, but most of the titles meant nothing to her. "I do not know these books, Don Julio."

"You will train yourself while you are working," Don Julio said. "Part of your job is to read the books you are selling."

Don Julio's strange notions teased her with the suspicion that he was making fun of her. Was he just another *ladino* who found Indians ridiculous? Yet his gentleness, his distance and detachment, which seemed in a contradictory way to bring him closer to her than the haughty self-assertion of other men, won her over. Their conversations assumed an unnerving intimacy; when offering advice, he slipped from the formal "*Usted*" into the "*tú.*" She was taken aback. She finally decided that, although he was too much of a gentleman to be impervious to the fact that she was an attractive young woman, he was

29

not trying to ruin her honour. He seemed curious about her, a reaction she had rarely encountered in anyone; the thrill of connection across barriers reminded her of how she had felt when she had met Ezequial.

The best customers were gringo professors who bought fat books on Guatemalan history that cost a month's wages each. They spoke to her in sometimes comical and self-important but surprisingly erudite Spanish about their *investigaciones*. Their interest in her culture reinforced her desire to learn their language: the language of people who were more open-minded than the *käk winaq*, as she called the *ladinos*. Sitting next to Eusebio on the bus back to the village at the end of the day, she bubbled with rage. The *ladinos* claimed that, being modern, they had the right to despise the Maya; but these gringos, who were more modern than Guatemalan *ladinos*, valued Mayan culture. She hurled herself into organizing the women from her church, and from the market — there was no market building then, just a collection of stalls in the dust next to the town hall. They worked for better schools, an enclosed market, Mayan-language instruction for children, a real clinic. Eusebio pleaded with her not to draw too much attention to herself. The war wasn't over; elsewhere in the country, Catholic activists were still being killed. In the eyes of the Army, Catholicism and Communism were related versions of collectivism; only individualistic Protestant Evangelicals were above suspicion.

She shared her insights about the customers with Don Julio. "It's true the gringos you're talking to are more open than the Guatemalan *burgués*," he said. "These are the good gringos. But the bad gringos, such as those who overthrew our government in 1954, are usually in power."

"Yes, Don Julio," she said, remembering his exile.

He gave her books to read, at first modern Guatemalan novels by Monteforte Toledo and Rey Rosa because these were the literary books she was most likely to sell. Then she read Rigoberta Menchú's memoirs, which seemed to have little to do with Menchú the public personality who journalists raged against in the newspapers — she had recently been awarded the Nobel Peace Prize, to the *ladinos'* horror — but was simply the story of all Mayan people during the worst days of the war. Yes, she thought, when she finished the book, this is what happens to us, even if the worst of it did not happen in this region.

Next Don Julio gave her the *Popol Vuh*, which had been translated into Spanish during the liberal government of the early 1950s. Amparo already knew these stories of the origins of life, having been told them in Cakchiquel by her grandmother. The pallid inadequacy of the Spanish translations of sacred language was complicated by the fact that, as Don Julio explained, the stories had been written down in Quiché. Yet after thinking about this, she decided that it was good to be reminded of the culture that all Mayan people shared. During the war, the Army did not ask whether people were Quiché or Mam or Q'eqchi or Cakchiquel before they killed them.

When Don Julio lent her a bilingual book of poems by a poet from Momostenango named Humberto Ak'abal, she was both exhilarated by the presence of the Quiché versions, which she could almost read, on the lefthand pages and vexed that all these famous promoters of Mayan culture spoke Quiché.

"Are there no Cakchiquels who write?" she asked. "No Mam or Tzutujil?"

"Maybe in the future. These could become languages that people will write in and speak on the radio and in government, or they could die out. It will depend on how organized Mayan people are after the war ends."

She had not thought about it in this way. His comment spurred her to feel that she must go beyond her frustrations with Mama — her narrow views, her shame in her language, her clothes, her very being — and see her life's broader horizons. She thirsted to drink down Don Julio's knowledge. Next morning, when he entered the bookstore, she was aware of his wiriness, of the gleam of his grey hair and the smack of his aftershave lotion. He walked towards her with a purposefulness which showed that he, too, was aware of a conversation left unfinished.

"I have something to ask you, Amparo."

She held her breath in fear. He had misinterpreted her need; he was about to make a proposal that would shame her. She struggled to remember whether she had told him about Eusebio.

"Have you heard of Francisco Marroquín University?" he said, tapping his fingers on the counter. "It's a private university in the capital. As a public service, this university has decided to create scholarships for Mayan students who are potential future community leaders. I would like to recommend you for one of these scholarships."

And so began the strangest episode of her life. Her parents did not understand why she, who had learned all that schools offered, could need to start studying again. The only university they had heard of was San Carlos, the public university, which was almost a war zone, where students were beaten and shot by soldiers, and even the professors used to disappear, their mutilated corpses turning up days later in ditches or garbage dumps. "No, Mama, it's not that kind of university. This is a peaceful place. It's where the rich people's children study."

"Then why do they want you?" Mama asked.

The question had crossed Amparo's mind as well. To receive the scholarship, she had to take a bus into the capital to an interview in a restaurant in Zone Ten. She had never set foot in this exclusive district of Guatemala City. Don Julio told her not to go to the interview in Western clothes. She must wear her village's traditional *huipil*, the *uq*, or Mayan skirt, and have her hair pulled back in a bun and held in place with a woven headband. She burst out laughing as he itemized the details. "This isn't a joke, Amparo," he said. "These people are searching for Mayan community leaders. You must look like a Mayan community leader."

The thought of entering Zone Ten in clothes she would not normally wear outside her village almost made her reject the offer. And, when she finally agreed and made the trip, in the crowded schoolbus into the capital she could feel people, many of them even poorer than she, sneering at her clothes. When she transferred in the chaos of Zone One to the muncipal bus that took her across the city, the disdain grew more potent. She hurried along the broad sidewalk of the divided Paseo de la Reforma, the grand boulevard whose name celebrated the decree that had given the *ladinos* the legal right to steal the Mayas' land, and reached the door of the restaurant. A tall doorman wearing a jacket with tails blocked her path and told her she could not enter.

She bowed her head. This was an elaborate joke; no one could really be inviting her to study at Francisco Marroquín University. Mama was right about the world and she was wrong. She hunched inside her *huipil*, wishing she could shed it. The sun's glare exposed her as she retreated down the sidewalk. The thought that she would have to ask directions to the bus back to Zone One mortified her. She was searching for someone who looked humble enough to reply to her query when a pudgy man in a suit ran towards her, his thin black tie flipped over his left shoulder by a gust of wind. "*¡Con permiso!* Are you Amparo

Ajuix? I'm *Licenciado* López. We're waiting for you in the restaurant."

He touched her arm as he guided her back down Paseo de la Reforma. She wasn't sure whether to take the gesture as courtly, or as a sign that he saw her as a clueless peasant. With his well-nourished mustache and florid cheeks, the man looked like a minor military official. His expression hardened as he paraded her past the hostile doorman and into the restaurant's hushed, carpeted interior. He seated her at a round table and introduced her to three men and a woman who were *licenciados* and an older man who was a *doctor*. She paid attention as she was introduced to these people; this did not prevent her from noticing the stares of the businessmen and the fine ladies, whose jewellery gleamed more brightly than their stricken white faces.

Into a sudden silence, *Licenciado* López said: "*Sakar. La utz a'wech?*"

His accent suggested that these might be the only words of Cakchiquel that he knew. "*Utz matiox,*" Amparo said. In Spanish she added: "Thank you very much for the invitation."

A man in a tuxedo hurried out of the back of the restaurant. He leaned over the *doctor*'s shoulder. Harsh whispers passed between them. " . . . Reputation of my establishment . . . decent people eat here . . . " He pulled himself upright and announced to the restaurant at large: "You did not warn me, sir! There will be no more reservations for the university!"

Applause pattered from the surrounding tables.

"The university is happy to go elsewhere," the *doctor* replied. "But for today we are here."

The *licenciada*, the only other woman at the table, met Amparo's eyes. "This is the Guatemala that we hope to change."

"I hope to change it, too," Amparo said. Their conversation took off. She did not finish the spicy *pepián* that the waiter brought her. A vision came to her of these *ladinos* as trapped inside their expensive clothes and their houses secured behind high walls. They were people imprisoned by privilege who were struggling to find a way out into the villages and the highlands, and all the wide expanse of the country that had been off-limits to them as long as the civil war had kept them barricaded in the capital. She grasped that her world was twice as large as theirs. Now that the war was ending and all of Guatemala would become one, they needed her. She began to speak with confidence about her community activities and how she had acquired her education. At the end of the meal they told her that they would like to award her the scholarship.

She carried the mood of that triumphant meal, where she took pleasure in the discomfort of the wealthy diners, into the first days of her studies. She ignored the fact that most students of Francisco Marroquín University shared little of their professors' idealism. She had imagined the university as a lofty, elevated place, yet it was sunken, as though in extreme discretion, into a walled-in bowl in the earth in the middle of the capital. Inside the guarded gates was a parking lot where students left the long, gleaming cars in which they drove to class. Immaculate parkland and two museums led to the steps of new buildings with broad corridors and large windows. Entering the cafeteria, she saw her first computers. A group of light-skinned young girls sat at a table holding enormous mugs of coffee in their hands. They chatted and typed, each on her own keyboard. The girls did not see her. Even later, when she sat next to them in *Licenciado* López's Guatemalan History course, which was the class she liked best, neither the girls nor the young men who were taking the course, noticed she was there. When *Licenciado* López lectured on the history of indigenous people, the young people displayed no awareness of the presence of indigenous students.

To get to class on time, Amparo woke up at 5:00 AM, rode the bus down the mountain to Antigua, made the hour-long trip from Antigua to the capital, then the almost equally long trip on the muncipal bus across Guatemala City from Zone One. She walked the last ten minutes to the university's gates. By the time she arrived her dress slacks and formal blouses, which felt dowdy by comparison with the clothes the girls with computers bought on their weekend shopping trips to Miami, were creased. She preferred creases to emulating the other three young indigenous women who had scholarships, all of whom wore *traje* as she had done during her interview. They were all Quiché. They spoke to each other in Quiché during breaks between classes. Amparo, who sat with them, could make out much of what they said but the hemmed-in world the young women had forged for themselves troubled her. If solitude was the meaning of Mayanness, she felt less Mayan than they. Was she, in the end, some sort of in-between person, deposited on an unstable middle ground by Mama's reluctance to teach her their ancestral culture? She was ashamed to admit to the indigenous women that there were subjects she could discuss more fluently in Spanish than in Cakchiquel, that she did not know how to measure time in *katuns*.

Eusebio, who had been her *novio* for five years, encouraged her in a flat voice. "I'm proud of you," he said, in a way that made his humility almost hurtful.

"You'll see more of me when I finish," she assured him.

"I want us to get married." It was Sunday afternoon. They were circling the village square holding hands, in the way that was approved of for acknowledged fiancés of firm religious belief.

36

"We'll get married as soon as I finish . . . "

"You'll be a different person then. You won't want to be with me."

"Eusebio, I want to be with you. That's not going to change." Yet as they rounded the corner of the square, the purple door of the house on the corner stared her in the face, reminding her of how much life could change.

She raised the question of marriage with the three Quichés. But their engagements were with Mayan men. Locked into the tight grid of traditional communities, they could never be expelled no matter how superior they became to the men with whom they had grown up. Again Amparo felt that their strength grew from narrowness. She was embarrassed to find that by starting this conversation she had put herself in a position where she had to concede that her fiancé was a poor, working class *ladino*. The other women stared at her. They understood being loyal to a Mayan community, they could imagine leaving the Mayan world to marry a man with a better education and more prospects — but to leave the community for a man who was neither wealthy nor Maya?

Next day, in the cafeteria, she sat by herself. Neither the *ladinos* nor the Quichés came to speak to her.

On Friday morning, exhausted and longing for the end of the week, she walked downhill towards the university gate beneath the pollution-heavy highland cloud. A woman who worked in the cafeteria walked ahead of her, carrying a bag over her shoulder. When the woman was within ten paces of the gate, two young men rushed towards her. They wore baseball caps pulled down over their eyes. Amparo's gaze locked on the long, silky dark hair hooked behind the ears of the man holding the pistol. The other man wielded a knife. They seized the woman, pushed the gun in her face, made a stab at the air with the knife, lifted her bag off her shoulder and, almost without breaking stride, plunged into the undergrowth on the other side of the street. The uniformed guards lounging around the booth behind the gate noticed what was happening only when it was too late.

The woman stared in front of her, frozen in silence. A howl of agony filled the roadway. Amparo rushed to her side.

"My money! My transistor radio! It took me months to save for that radio!"

"Tranquila, señora. You're safe, it's all right."

"My radio! My radio! How will I hear the voice of Jesus Christ without my radio?"

Two guards, Galil rifles levelled, pounced out into the roadway in combat posture and entered the bushes uttering threatening grunts. Amparo accompanied the woman past the museums and the young people chatting in the parking lot. She left her at the door of the cafeteria, giving her ten quetzales to buy herself lunch, even though the other employees were almost certain to offer her leftover food. During her classes, she felt trapped inside an invisible skin. In spite of her Quiché classmates' invocation of traditional religion and something they called, in Spanish, *la cosmovisión maya,* the presence of Xpiyacoc and Ixmucane grew fainter. *Licenciado* López's voice, as he gave his lecture, failed to pry her free from the speechless moment that had gripped the cafeteria employee during the seconds after she was robbed.

By the end of the day she had decided not to return to the university. That afternoon, when the bus from the capital juddered into the market in Antigua, she stepped down onto the hard ruts. Her head lowered, she walked towards the park.

Don Julio was in the bookstore chatting with a new employee, a young girl Amparo didn't recognize. He grew animated at her arrival. Amparo interrupted him in a muted voice to tell her of her decision.

He grew silent. "I can see you're not going to change your mind. You haven't come here to ask me to persuade you to give it one more week?" He chewed his lip. "This tension's always going to be there. To make your culture advance you must give up part of it. If you live your life as the mother of many children, you'll maintain your customs in a state of weakness. And in the future that's not going to work. Your children will go to the *maquilas* or to the north and your culture will be lost. It's only by compromising with the modern world that you'll spare part of that richness." He shook his head. "Believe me, I didn't used to think this way. I believed in total resistance. But that's not going to be possible anymore — "

She stared into his face until it blurred before her eyes and the books arranged cover-out on the wall behind him became a tapestry of indecipherable colours, a pattern on a *huipil* whose village of origin she could not identify. She remembered how she used to hunger for his conversation. Behind his words she felt his wounded disappointment; his inability to express this emotion directly, his need to turn it into an intellectual argument, deepened her disillusionment. Over his shoulder, she saw the slender girl staring at them. She said: "If I keep going there I'm going to lose my fiancé. I can't imagine marrying anyone else. He treats me well. So few men are like that."

He bowed his head. He couldn't disprove feelings. She thanked him with lavish formality for his interest in her. She left El Tesoro. She had not set foot in the store again.

That Sunday afternoon as she and Eusebio circled the park, she told him of her decision. She saw him absorbing the news. She had to wait only a few moments for him to ask her the question he had asked her once before, when they had been *novios* for only a few months. "Amparo, will you marry me?"

"*Ri nuwuchejil!*" she exclaimed. My husband! Observing his bewildered reaction, she remembered that he did not understand her language.

FIVE

S HE WALKED UP THE STEPS of El Tesoro for the first time
in four years. Ten days ago she had phoned and asked to
speak to Don Julio. When she introduced herself, there was a
long silence. In a subdued voice, he asked her whether she had
many children. Only one so far, she told him, and a second
one on the way. "I think two will be enough." She felt a twist
of discomfort. She told him that the handicrafts she sold in
the village market no longer made ends meet. Don Julio made
a commiserating comment about how expensive the country
had become. He could not offer her work at El Tesoro, but if
he heard of something he would let her know. Having accepted
this polite refusal as a rebuff, she was surprised when the phone
rang the next morning and she heard his voice telling her that
the nuns at Escuela San Fernando were looking for an educated
woman of strong Catholic faith to teach kindergarten and the
first year of primary school.

As she entered the bookstore, the shelves of face-out covers
encircled her. She hadn't read a book since Sandra was born.

"May I help you, señora?"

"Yes, is Don Julio in, please? My name is Amparo Ajuix."

The young woman, who was sliding out from behind the
counter, paused. Amparo traced the fall of her long dark hair
to the unexpected challenge of her lucid eyes. This was the
girl who had been working in her place the day she told Don

Julio that she was leaving the university. Four years had lent her waistline a relaxed fullness. She examined Amparo's body, her merciless scrutiny making Amparo feel like a pregnant teenager.

Leaning around a corner, the girl called down the narrow passage between the bookstore and the souvenir shop: "Julio, there's a lady here who wants to speak with you."

The girl addressed Don Julio as "*tú*."

"Amparo!" Don Julio emerged from the passage. "What a pleasure to see you!" Shaking her hand, he addressed her with the formal pronoun. She heard his restraint as a reprimand to the girl's boldness. "You've met my wife?"

Amparo extended her hand. "*Mucho gusto, señora.*"

The girl's loose smile exposed the large Mayan teeth behind her rouged *ladino* lips. "*Mucho gusto.*"

"Sonia came to work for me after you left. And she stayed!" Don Julio's laughter shook his frame into that of a stranger. His hair was white, his thinness no longer looked trim or compact. Living with this girl had coarsened him. Could Sonia be his equal in anything? Anything except the one thing made obvious by her taut designer bluejeans and the high breasts tightening the lines of her sweater? Don Julio had fallen prey to the miserable obsession that all men shared. A conflicted pride in Eusebio's moral behaviour surged up through her irritation.

"Thank you so much for helping me find work, Don Julio . . . "

"I only hope you can continue working there once your child is born."

He thought she would quit again. She was doomed to disappoint him, once more making him look bad for having supported her. "I will speak to Sister Consuelo about continuing to work after the child is born." She stepped forward, emboldened by an awareness that Sonia's coldness contained a shiver of insecurity: she did not have a child. Married to an older man, she might never have children. Amparo felt her position strengthen. "This child — "

But Don Julio had already begun to speak. "Yes, you should talk to Sister Consuelo. Perhaps she will find a solution."

She sought out his eyes behind his glasses, convinced that he was talking about more than holding onto her job. For an instant he held her gaze, igniting their old complicity. He, too, she saw, felt the return of their secret understanding, more powerful because neither of them had crossed these social barriers with anyone else. She had been the first Mayan woman he had got to know; he was her only friend among the *burguesía*.

The sensation passed. Don Julio, shrugging his shoulders with a motion that carried him into the doorway where the girls serving at the tables passed back and forth behind him, said: "And your husband?"

"He's a social worker for an NGO. They run a drop-in centre for people living on the street. He would like to do something else, but he lacks a high school diploma."

"He's lucky to have an educated wife."

Amparo struggled to smile. She struggled not to cry.

"Julio," Sonia said. "We have to pay the suppliers."

"Thank you very much for your help, Don Julio." Amparo shook his hand. She spotted an enormous gringo leafing through a book with a photograph of a Mayan village on the cover and wished she could ask him if he needed help. She stumbled into the street.

SIX

S HE WALKED WITHOUT A DESTINATION, blinking against the sunlight. As her composure returned, she passed the San Pedro Church. On the street in front of the steps, a young priest was blessing a *ladino* family's new car. The priest finished his oration and began to sprinkle water on the car's hood. A group of pale, bulky tourists with cameras came around the corner. The priest, growing nervous, rushed the blessing. He cast the water about in haste, looking terrified that he might become an attraction to be photographed. The sight steadied Amparo. Those who accused her of backwardness were themselves seen as backward by others. Which meant that the idea of backwardness had no meaning. Pausing in front of the church, she crossed herself.

She walked to the market and took the bus back up the mountainside to the village. She got out two blocks north of the park. At the house on the corner, the purple door opened and a modest figure in a long skirt emerged. Amparo started to turn away. But it was too late: Raquel called her name.

Amparo crossed the street. Raquel gave her a hug and invited her in. "Why don't I see you anymore?"

"I'm so busy." She stared across the lintel and took a quick look over her shoulder at the passengers dispersing from the idling schoolbus.

"And expecting another child. Come in and tell me about it."

Amparo glimpsed Doña María's daughter emerging from the market, carrying her baby. Hoping the girl had not spotted her, she slipped into the house and closed the door behind her.

"I don't have to start cooking yet," Raquel said. "Jorge won't come back until late."

Amparo remained standing on the tiles.

"Come in!" Raquel said, tugging at her sleeve. "Why can't we talk like we used to?"

"I have to go home. My mother's been looking after Sandra all day. I'm teaching little girls at Escuela San Fernando. As I'm expecting, I tire quickly."

Raquel, thin and dark, spurned adornment. She wore long skirts in Western style, and did not speak Cakchiquel even with her mother; her preacher had told her Indian dialects were shameful. She stared at Amparo with the sympathy that made her company so enticing. "Amparo, you always had time for everyone: your husband, your work, the Savings Club, your church. And you had time to talk as well." She straightened up. "You're not yourself."

"Eusebio — doesn't — want — me — to — talk — to — you."

A horrible sense of everything being wrong swamped her like nightfall. It was wrong to betray her husband by criticizing him, wrong to bare her unhappiness to Raquel rather than to Sister Consuelo. Accustomed to howling about her discomforts in church before unordained upstart preachers, surrounded by co-worshippers who moaned out loud about the sins they had committed before being saved, Raquel could only trivialize Amparo's pain. The secrets they had shared in the past had been discarded like corn husks.

45

"Why doesn't he want you to talk to me? Because of my religion? Amparo, we've never let this come between us." She shook her head, her large eyes looking sad yet inquisitive. No doubt she had found new confidantes to whom anything Amparo revealed would be passed along.

She must not say a word.

"Let me get you a handkerchief."

Raquel disappeared through the kitchen into the back room. Amparo felt marooned in the small, silent house, trying to contain sobs that were too big for her body. A poster over the sink, emblazoned with English words in yellow lettering, showed a crowd of thousands stretching away before a preacher staring heavenwards against the backdrop of a tilted cross. Raquel, bringing her a cloth handkerchief, said: "It's pretty, no? It's a gift from missionaries who visited our church. It shows a great crusade for souls that took place in the United States." Watching Amparo rub her eyes, Raquel said: "Your Pope never gets crowds like that!"

"The Pope gets bigger crowds than any of your preachers. Didn't you see the pictures on television when he was in Mexico?" Trying to calm her anger, she reminded herself of the affinities that used to weld her to Raquel: active women who had exercised careful judgement to spare themselves the misery of unfaithful or drunken husbands, they had selected men who were calmer and more modest than they. They used to giggle about their quiet husbands over Raquel's kitchen table.

"Your Pope," Raquel said, "distracts people from direct communication with Jesus Christ."

This was a conversation Amparo preferred to avoid. She felt little warmth towards Pope John Paul II, who disdained the poor and offered solace to their oppressors. But he was still the successor to St. Peter. When the Pope had visited Guatemala,

46

thugs from Raquel's church had run around Antigua defacing the posters that announced his visit by drawing black horns above John Paul II's ears and scrawling "*The Anti-Christ*" across his forehead. "Your church doesn't even have priests," she retorted. "It's the blind leading the blind."

They never used to talk about religion. It had been the subject furthest from their long, intimate afternoons.

Raquel gave her arm a glancing touch. "Are you sure you won't sit down? I've got a pie that Ezequial brought from Comalapa."

Amparo handed her the handkerchief. "I have to go home."

"Now what's wrong?" Raquel said, leaving the handkerchief dangling in front of her. "Aren't I allowed to mention my brother's name?"

"A married woman does not want to hear about her ex-fiancé." Amparo pushed the crumpled handkerchief into Raquel's hands. She heard Raquel's breath trembling. "I have to go."

"Come back. Bring Sandra with you. We can talk."

You can talk, Amparo thought. That was what she feared. News spread through the village in a second, in spite of the barriers between Catholics and Evangelicals.

She submitted to Raquel's embrace and stepped out of the house into the dusty park. Through the broad doorway of the market, she saw that most of the stalls had closed. The bougainvillea's luxuriance made no impact on her as she walked home. She followed the long curve of the dirt street towards the gate of the compound.

"Amparo!" Doña María's sliding gait made her look almost crippled. The leather strap of her right sandal was clinging by a thread. "Amparo. I've come from talking to your mother. You know that she and I were neighbours when I was a girl."

"Yes, Doña María," Amparo said, realizing that in Cakchiquel she accepted as ritualized greetings phrases that in Spanish sounded like repetitions. Her head bowed, she said a formal: "*La utz ab'anon?* How is your health?"

"*Matiox, matiox.*" Doña María scrutinized Amparo. "*Ret b'ison.* You look sad." When Amparo refused to rise to this, the old woman said: "I hoped to find you at home. I wanted to talk to you about the proposals for schools in Cakchiquel."

"Yes, with the Peace Accords teaching in our school will be in Cakchiquel in the early years." She took a step forward. "The members of our church have written to the government to request that the language of instruction be changed by next year."

Doña María's expression folded in on itself in leathery distaste. The rose-coloured blossoms over her shoulder brightened the dusty street. "Your church . . . " Of the two Cakchiquel words for church, she chose the half-Spanish one that sounded disparaging: *ChichoDios,* God's car. "Amparo, we don't want our children to be backward — "

"Our children will approach Spanish with more confidence if they can write in their own language and know their *history.*" She enunciated the final term with particular force — *ojer tz'ij,* "ancient words" — to refute the way that this conversation about public matters was obliging them to stud their Cakchiquel with Spanish expressions. In Spanish history was an *historia,* a story like any other you might tell, full of fibs and exaggerations; in Cakchiquel it was words transmitted from ancient times.

"That's fine for you, who live in a compound," Doña María said. "My husband sows corn. We can't teach our children to read and write Spanish because we barely write it ourselves. Where will our children learn, if not in school?"

"But Doña María, you don't send your boys to school!"

48

"My daughter was the best student in her year. Imagine where she would be if she had studied in some dialect!"

"Maybe she would have understood her position in this country well enough not to have a baby at fourteen," Amparo said.

"And you think you are such a fine married woman!"

In spite of herself, Amparo took a step forward. The volume of her body hindered her. "What do you mean, Doña María?"

They glared at each other. Doña María's disdain filled her with fear. Had she glimpsed Doña María's *nahual*: the secret animal each person carried inside them, who came to their rescue in moments of distress on the condition that the animal's identity not be revealed? Doña María was a poisonous snake. "Understand her position in this country!" Doña María grumbled. "The Army was right. Priests and Communists are the same. *Los curas son comunistas y los comunistas son curas.*"

"Is that what your gringo missionaries say when they come and take your money?"

"Who are you to criticize us for contributing to our church? You, with your fancy altars and your incense! My friend Jesus Christ drove the moneychangers from the temple, but you meet in the church to count your money."

"You may join us," Amparo said, "as soon as you send your boys to school."

"I'm not going to send them to school in some backward dialect so that you can keep your compound while my family sows corn!" Doña María spoke in Cakchiquel. The only Spanish words in the sentence were "backward dialect."

"Doña María — "

The older woman turned away and shuffled down the street, favouring her disintegrating right sandal. She stopped and turned around. "Who are you to criticize my daughter,

49

when your sister Yolanda sits on park benches in Antigua with gringo men?"

Amparo turned towards the metal gate. Her big body wearied her. She felt a treacherous dash of shame at the child that was pushing its way into her life. As she reached the gate, her mother came to the door and let her into the yard, preceding her across the hard dirt with her seized-up stride. Mama had never complained about all the children she had borne. Amparo read a reproach in her mother's kind, enduring features, the grey hair that hung in straight hanks to her broad, pitched-back shoulders, her *huipil* with its motifs declaring her citizenship of this village and her heavy *uq* scattered with squiggles of the wool she was carding at a bench in the yard.

"How's Sandra?" Amparo asked, alerted to her own maternal duties.

"She's in the house. Eusebio came and got her. He asked where you were."

"I'm here." She avoided Mama's questioning gaze. "I ran into Doña María. 'Your mother and I were neighbours when I was a girl,'" she said, imitating Doña María's voice.

"That was before she married that man. *La ma' la' nurayij nükum ya',*" Mama said, repeating a phrase Amparo had heard women speak too many times before: The man likes to drink liquor. Eusebio remained the rare husband to whom this phrase did not apply. For a moment she longed to rush into the house, certain that Eusebio would hug and kiss her, and everything would be the way it was before. " . . . No wonder his sons have to work in the *milpa* instead of going to school . . . He was always a difficult man, even before *xepolpotijkï!*"

Whenever a family in the village was converted to Evangelical Protestantism, Mama referred to them as having been flipped upside down. Since Doña María, her husband and

50

their children had been flipped by a pudgy man from Alabama who wore a purple T-shirt with a white cross on the back, and encouraged his followers to daub their houses with purple paint, Mama had barely spoken to them.

"Did she talk to you about the school?"

"Yes," Mama said. "In the past I thought like her. But now you tell me that you can write in Cakchiquel. Well, if we can write in this language, maybe I should have taught it to you better."

Engulfed by her mother's shame, Amparo took a step towards her. Mama returned to her bench and resumed carding the wool. Once her hands had slipped into an easy rhythm, she said: "I told Doña María I didn't understand the idea of a school in Cakchiquel, but that if it was what my children wanted for their children I wasn't going to argue."

"Two hundred thousand people died to make this possible. We have to respect their sacrifice."

Mama continued to card. At last she looked up. "Amparo, you think too much about big problems. Go cook supper for your husband!"

SEVEN

"MAMA!" SANDRA FLUNG HER ARMS around Amparo's knees, hobbling her. "Nana was teaching me to weave!"

"What a good girl!" She wondered how much of her infancy Sandra would remember when she grew up. The corrugated zinc roof felt too low overhead.

"Come watch television, Sandra." Eusebio clicked the remote until a program for children appeared. "Mama and Papa have to talk. Then Mama'll make supper."

Amparo glanced at him. She had grown accustomed to evenings when they did not talk. "Where's Inés?" she asked.

"In the market, closing your stall." He laid his hand on the bedroom door.

She followed him into the room. Eusebio closed the door and stood in front of it. "You were at Ezequial's house."

She twisted on her toes.

"Seeing your ex-fiancé . . . " He looked at her with a stoic, wounded expression. "I asked your mother where you were and Doña María tells me you're at Ezequial's house!"

"Doña María!"

"Yes, I had to hear it from her."

Now any reply she made would sound false. "Ezequial wasn't there, Eusebio. I wouldn't have gone in if he had been. I was talking to Raquel."

"Oh Raquel. She's the perfect pretext, isn't she? Pious Raquel. She was the excuse you used when you started seeing Ezequial, wasn't she?"

"I only did that once, Eusebio. I was eighteen years old and even then I realized I'd made a mistake. I went and told my mother the truth."

"The truth." Eusebio sighed. Yielding his grip on the door, he paced a circle through the gloom. She watched him pass their wedding photograph and the tortoise shell they'd found on the beach at Monterrico during their honeymoon weekend. A photograph of his late mother dressed for church showed her *ladino* finery offset by features that were as Mayan as those of anyone in Amparo's family. His large upper body weighed him down like a sack of corn. "It would be good to hear more of the truth in this house."

"You know the truth, Eusebio."

"I'm afraid I do."

"Eusebio!" For an instant she could have shaken him by the ears. "How can you say such things to the woman who is carrying your child?" She looked him in the eyes. "*Your* child, Eusebio."

Eusebio kept pacing. She longed to tell him of Don Julio's young wife: they used to share such delicious news. The worst part was knowing she was lucky. Wives in Santa María, where the women loved to marry soldiers, had been killed by their husbands on less evidence than this. She felt gratitude, then resentment: why should she be grateful to him for not acting like a *militar*?

She realized that Mama must have been present when Doña María had told him his wife was at her ex-fiancé's house.

Eusebio sat down on the bed. "Amparo, what have you done to me? For you I moved to this village, I became part of your family — "

Part of a Mayan family, he meant. For her he had gone to live with a bunch of Indians. Perhaps he should remember that his family, proud *ladinos* though they might be, had eaten rice and beans for breakfast, rice and beans for lunch and rice and beans for supper. By settling in an Indian village he had moved into a decent house built by her father and shared meals of vegetables, avocado, and chicken provided by her family's hard work.

"I have to cook Sandra's supper." She struggled to contain the shudder in her voice. "Soon we will have two children . . . "

"No!" The cry punctuated his sobbing with a breathy silence. "Amparo — "

She stifled the impulse to throw herself into his arms, throttled the desire to slap him across the face. She stood with her feet apart on the tiles. The windowless bedroom felt too small; her marriage was too small. This compound, where she must lie to her mother about her marriage, penned her in. She had worked in many different jobs, yet none of them had released the energy that swelled inside her with more force than this child. So many possibilities untapped, and now this hateful guilt that tracked her everywhere.

Eusebio hunched on the bed with his face in his hands, the label of his T-shirt poking up like a miniature flag of surrender. How glossy with sweat the hair on the back of his neck had felt beneath her hands when they had made the child!

The baby's strangeness shook her like a chasm opening in the earth. She could only glimpse how this person she had never met would perceive his world. Again she felt excluded, isolated in her own home. The love she felt for the baby inside her filled her with guilt and worry. Her place in this household returned in hard specifics that blossomed in her mind: *Re'n pa nu wochó, re'n q'o ri nu akual, nip'a ri nu ch'i'p, ri nu akual rojo yi'wa* . . . She was in her home, she had a child and a youngest of the family on the way and her child wanted to eat. These were the facts. Nothing could change them.

She opened the door and stepped into the living room. Sandra darted up from the television. "Were you bad, Mama?"

"Of course I wasn't bad. Adults can't be bad." She stroked Sandra's hair.

"Papa tells me to go to my room when I'm bad."

She regarded her daughter's narrow shoulders and long straight hair. "Papa didn't *tell* me to go to my room. We had something to talk about. A grown-up conversation."

"Is Papa feeling bad? He wasn't feeling bad before. Did you make Papa feel bad?"

"Sandra, *por el amor de Dios!*" She filled a pot with water and hunted for matches to light the stove. She motioned for Sandra to help her. Aware of the television babbling in Spanish, she asked in Cakchiquel: "Did Nana speak to you in our language today?"

"*Ja!*" Sandra confirmed.

"*Enchi' q'o ri ixtën?* Where's the servant girl?"

"*Raja xipa* . . . " Sandra's Cakchiquel sputtered out. "She came in while you and Papa were talking."

Amparo knocked on the girl's door and told her to start working. Inés stared at her for a moment, her large eyes afraid, then entered the kitchen and heated the rice. She pared the meat from two legs of a chicken and fried it in a corner of the pan across which the paste of *frijoles* was spreading. Watching her work, Amparo sectioned an avocado with strokes made sluggish by her puffy wrists.

They ate in silence. Sandra stared around the table. Amparo felt furious with her whole family. The child in her womb tugged at her heart, commanding gentleness towards it alone.

When she had finished eating she left the table and closed the bedroom door behind her, wishing she had asked Don Julio to recommend a book. On her shelf, next to the crowded photograph of her siblings, she had a Monteforte Toledo novel published under the liberal government of the early 1950s. The novel was about an idealistic *ladino* who was sent as a doctor to a Mayan village and fell in love with a Mayan woman. She had started the novel once before. Discovering that she remembered the first few chapters, she flipped to the middle, to a painful scene where the doctor's family came from the capital to visit him in the village. It had been so long since she had read anything longer than articles in the *Prensa Libre* that she wrestled for a few minutes with the act of concentration, with closing out the grumble of voices and the clang of pots from the next room, resigning herself to the fact that the book was in Spanish and the author's obsession was the hypocrisy of *ladinos* who knew little about their country. As she read, her mood changed. She had forgotten the magical self-enlargement of reading. Laying the book aside at the end of the chapter, she thought about how, during the worst years of the civil war in the highlands, Maya caught with books — any book, even the Bible — were executed. She chided herself for not taking advantage of the privilege of having books, now that peace had come, when many Mayan brothers and sisters had paid with their lives for this right.

Eusebio entered the bedroom. "Amparo, I'm not going to take this any more. My daughter just asked me if I was bad. Me! When I've done nothing but look like a fool — "

"Is that what you told her? That you looked like a fool? You told our daughter — "

"I didn't tell her anything. I told her to get ready for bed. I told her she was being bold." His voice dropped. "Just like her mother."

Once he had used this phrase to tease her. The shadow of the novel cushioned her with the fictional family's torments. She saw their foolishness, lighted up against the backdrop of that of the family in the novel. They might quarrel all night, but in the end they wouldn't understand each other better, be any different, or any less married, than they were right now. The realization made her bolder. "Don't you ever say anything like that to Sandra again," she replied, knowing that her casual tone would heighten his fury.

"I'll speak to her the way I want to! ¡*Carajo*! I'm the head of this family. I'm not going to take this any more!"

She sidled to within a few centimetres of his face. "What aren't you going to take any more, Eusebio?"

"You deceiving me in front of the whole village. You've made me look like a fool."

The smell of his sweat filled her nostrils, her pores. *Dios*, this is Eusebio, my Eusebio and he really believes . . . he's really incensed. In her disregard she had drifted into a fast-flowing mountain current, and now she was being swept down the mountainside. She prayed to the heart of the sky and the heart of the earth and the wisdom of their eternal union.

Eusebio was shouting at her so loudly and quickly that she could not absorb his rage. He seized her wrist until it burned. She could throw him off, she could flee out the door and across the compound to her father's house, but the moment she did that, time would stop. As soon as a woman fled, her marriage was over. She lived alone for the rest of her life; her children were taunted, other women accused her of tempting their husbands. Then she grew old and became a burden. If she ran, her life was lost. Eusebio, unconstrained by a village or a Mayan community, could return to Antigua and find another woman. The unfairness made her veins throb harder. She struggled against him and threw him off. Sweating, they stared at each other. They were almost as they had been when they made the child. "I haven't ruined your life, Eusebio," she said in a low rush, determined that Sandra would not overhear her. "But you're about to ruin it. There's nothing wrong here except your *machista* stupidity."

Part of her wanted to be hit. She, who advised the young women in the Cakchiquel Women's Savings Club, should know better than to feel in the thud of a husband's fist evidence of his devotion. Many times she had told young girls that this was not a respectful foundation for a marriage. Yet too often beating was passion turned on its head, promising the rebirth of intimacy: she struggled to snuff out the lure of this falsehood. She tried to count the weeks since they had last come together as man and wife; her body craved the weight of his hands.

Her neediness gutted her anger. She lay on the bed, desperate that Sandra not hear her tears.

Eusebio was silent. His hands lifted and fell next to the brass studs of the pockets of his bluejeans. She remembered giggling with Raquel about how, seeing farther than other girls, they had chosen fiancés who would allow them to arrange their weddings at an appropriate time rather than having them dictated by the frenzied ticking of a nine-month clock. But they had failed like other women. Raquel, still childless beneath the eyes of the village, waited for quiet Jorge to return from ever-longer days at work. And she —

"First you betray me," Eusebio said, "then you insult me." He paused, as though an idea had just occurred to him. When he looked up, she saw a tired ghost of his old boyish glinting, "I'm going to sleep on the couch tonight. I can't stay here. I can't take any more of this."

Her lips felt dry. "Will you put Sandra to bed, or should I?"

EIGHT

SHE WOKE IN THE MORNING to the heat of the child in her stomach. Her next thought was for Sandra.

She got out of bed, dressed, and opened the bedroom door. Eusebio, curled in front of the television, glanced at her. He rolled over, shrugging his shoulders in his white T-shirt as he set aside the blanket, embroidered with rabbit-god motifs by Amparo's grandmother. He looked more unshaven than usual. "Come back into the bedroom before Sandra sees you," she whispered.

"Was Papa bad?"

Amparo turned around, swept her daughter off her feet and covered her face with kisses. She carried her back to her bed. "Papa was feeling ill last night," she said. "He didn't want to keep Mama awake . . . We don't have to talk about it to anyone."

"You mean to Nana?"

Amparo's grip faltered. Would this be Sandra's earliest memory: her mother coaching her to hide her parents' arguments from her grandmother? She used to make lists of the lessons she would teach her children. Honesty had been near the top . . . But then she had also planned to speak to them in Cakchiquel. "*Anchi jat jech'ël?*" she said in exasperation. "What makes you so twisted?"

Sandra burst into tears. Amparo hugged her, lifting her off the bed. "*Mijita, mi pobre niña . . .* " She caressed Sandra's back, continuing to murmur in Spanish. "It's all right, I promise."

Sandra's crying stopped. In a clear voice, she said: "If I don't tell Nana that Papa slept on the couch, will you bring me something from Antigua?"

"No, I will not bring you anything from Antigua and you will not tell Nana. You will be a good girl and do as Mama tells you."

Sandra burst into tears. "Papa! I want Papa . . . !"

Amparo got up and left the bedroom. "You deal with her."

Forty minutes later, as she led a scrubbed, contrite Sandra into the yard of the compound, she was aware of the reflection of her own drained features in her mother's face. "Is Eusebio going to Antigua with you?"

"No, Mama, his work starts later."

Her mother spared her a quick look, then turned her attention to her granddaughter. Like she herself, Mama felt that she had to make life better for Sandra.

Through an open window, Amparo could hear Esperanza's husband talking to their children over breakfast. Her brother and his wife, who lived in the house in the corner of the compound, were opening their shutters. Papa was away on an overnight container pick-up to the Atlantic Coast. As Amparo started towards the steel gate, Yolanda appeared from her parents' house, looking too buoyant for the early hour. Her hair was thick, her face gleamed. Seventeen, Amparo thought. Yolanda wore a blue dress that fell to just above her knees. The dress was too short. Where had Yoli got the money for a dress like that?

They went out the gate together and down the street towards the square.

"We'll all be proud when you graduate," Amparo said, remembering the spontaneity that used to tingle between them when Yolanda was a little girl bursting with questions for her big sister. She drew a quick breath to keep up with the girl's brisk stride. As the idling Bluebird schoolbus came into sight, Amparo glimpsed the *ayudante* waving Yolanda's friends on board. "Yoli, you don't have a gringo boyfriend?"

"A gringo?" Yolanda looked puzzled. "I don't know many gringos. Lots of gringos come into the café, but most of them hardly speak Spanish."

Her stride accelerated again. When had Yolanda become taller than her? "You know you have to be careful, Yoli."

"Amparo, how old do you think I am? Just because I'm not like you . . . "

Yolanda hurried away to join her friends. Amparo got on the bus and sat by herself next to a window.

At the Escuela San Fernando, the girls ran across the schoolyard, their black braids and tartan skirts bouncing. Amparo wondered how many of them had parents who argued. Their bright faces, as gleeful as those of piglets, cried out in playfulness as though crying out in pain.

At the end of the day she sat down on a bench in the sunlight, breathing in the aroma of bougainvillea and dust. She thought of the centuries of nuns who had taught children here and prayed in peace in the cells that overlooked the courtyard, the cobblestoned streets, and the volcanoes, then turned her gaze towards Sister Consuelo, who came out of the building and sat down next to her. The sunlight exposed pleats in the corners of the nun's eyes that suggested that this young woman, who Amparo had taken to be in her late twenties, was in fact a decade older. She risked a confession of weakness. "I'm tired. The child is tiring me."

"That's what my sister says. Her children tire her most before they are born."

"They can tire you a lot after they're born, too." Amparo's surprise took a moment to register. "You have a sister who has children, Sister Consuelo?"

"Yes, in Jaen, in Andalusia." The nun paused; Amparo sensed that she was inhaling the volcanic odour of the dust. How different her Andalusia must smell! "My sister did not have a vocation. She is a very beautiful woman. When we were girls, the boys . . . "

A vision formed in Amparo's mind of a past in which Sister Consuelo had been not a nun, but a plain girl who watched in envy as her beautiful sister received visits from boys. Confiding in a nun would be no betrayal of her husband because a nun was the bride of Christ.

"Her path was that of holy matrimony and children. Mine was that which you see."

"Sister Consuelo, I have many problems in my family."

"You must pray to God . . . " As though perceiving the precipice over which Amparo felt herself hanging, Sister Consuelo changed course. "Do you wish to talk about these problems?"

"Yes, yes." She felt hot with fear, but it was too late to retreat. She glanced around the empty courtyard. Two nuns stood on the shadowed back steps; in the far corner the old grounds-keeper was raking the dirt with his reed broom.

Sister Consuelo got to her feet. When they passed out of the sunlight into the shadow of the convent, Amparo lifted her head and found her eyes brimming with tears. She stumbled on the steps. Sister Consuelo slid an arm around her waist. She drew a long breath, then the arm was gone and Amparo felt the light reproof of the nun's austerity, yet a reproof that reassured her because it meant that God would absolve her for the words she was going to utter about her husband.

They entered the small bare room with the crucifix on the wall. Sister Consuelo shut the door, closing out the smells and voices and hot sunlight. Amparo concentrated on the presence of God. She had rarely felt such a cool, pure Catholicism; Ixmucane and Xpiyacoc receded. She wondered whether Sister Consuelo's cell resembled this office. Facing the nun across the bare wooden table, she said: "My husband does not believe that our child — the child who will soon be born — is his."

"Have you given him reason to believe this?"

"No! Of course not!" Tears ripped through her.

Sister Consuelo's face was unforgiving. "Are you certain, Amparo, that none of your actions has been open to misinterpretation?"

She had expected more sympathy. She tried to examine her conscience, to earn God's compassion. "My husband is a good man." Sister Consuelo was a nun, but she was a European; she must not think that Eusebio was drunken or unfaithful. "He asks only to be a good father. He works helping street children, he brings home the little money he makes, he cares for our daughter, he does not drink — "

As she gulped for breath, trying to hold back her tears, Sister Consuelo said: "You have not answered my question."

" — but he has fallen prey to a terrible deception."

"Why did this happen, Amparo?"

Amparo stared at the crucifix over the door.

"Before I met my husband," she said, "I had another fiancé. When I was eighteen years old, my brother would go to see his friend Ezequial. They would walk around the village together. Ezequial has a sister, Raquel. Even though their family is Evangelical and we are Catholics, Raquel became my best

64

friend. We talked about all the things that girls talk about. When my brother and I left our compound, we would tell our mother that we were going to visit Ezequial and Raquel, and she would let us go. Then one day, as we were walking along the path that leads up the hill behind our village, my brother and I exchanged positions. He walked with Raquel and I walked with Ezequial. At first I felt sorry for Ezequial because he had a bad leg. I could see he was a good person and I admired him because he never complained about his limp. That was the beginning of my feelings for him . . . of his becoming my fiancé. My mother never suspected because I would say I was going to visit Raquel . . . "

Sister Consuelo shook her head. "How people ruin themselves for the illusion of earthly love!"

"I was only eighteen," Amparo said, "but I knew this was wrong. After two weeks, I went to my mother and told her the truth. I said that Ezequial was my fiancé, that we went for walks and held hands and talked about the future. My mother said that if I married him I would have to convert to Evangelicalism, and that I should think about this very carefully."

"You put an end to this folly?"

"Not immediately. I was studying, I was working. Ezequial asked me a lot about my beliefs. I felt like forbidden fruit. He had been brought up to believe that Catholics were evil."

"Meeting you showed him the falsehood of his ways."

"It showed him that Catholics could be good people. I didn't change his mind. He insisted that if we married I must convert. After a year I realized I couldn't become an Evangelical. I found it . . . undignified. And so I told Ezequial I couldn't marry him."

"You did this without compromising yourself?" Sister Consuelo's gaze was relentless.

"Without compromising myself," Amparo replied. "It was just sympathy on my part and curiosity on his. We were young and mistook these feelings for love." Seeing Sister Consuelo flinch at the word "love," Amparo pressed forward: "After this, I decided to devote my sympathy to my own community, to promote my culture and help the women in my village."

"Have you told your husband about Ezequial?"

"Yes." A stirring of confusion made her realize how calm she had grown. Her gratitude towards the nun backed up into impatience. "When I met Eusebio in Antigua and he became my fiancé, I used to stay here after work on Friday evenings and Eusebio and I would go to dances in the Pensativo football stadium. We danced all night, but we respected each other. We never went off into the dark together like some couples. There were no buses back to the village when the dances ended, but there were boys who had cars. Eusebio would walk me to a car. You wouldn't believe it — seven or eight young people would squeeze into a two-door car and we would groan and scream all the way up the mountain!"

"That was more immoral than anything you did with your fiancé."

"Yes, they were sinful car rides!" Sister Consuelo's fixed expression curtailed Amparo's laughter. Taken aback, Amparo thought: now that she thinks men like me, that I'm like her beautiful sister, she's going to find it harder to forgive me.

"Girls sitting on the laps of total strangers!"

"*Bueno*, people we knew from the village." Amparo searched for a way to change the subject. "I told my mother about my evenings with Eusebio. I said she could have complete confidence in me. The only time she was nervous was when our church group made a trip to El Salvador. I went as Eusebio's fiancé. I sat next to him on the bus. The nuns who accompanied us frowned on this. One of them told my mother that I was the only girl who had sat next to a boy. It was true, but the boys and the girls spent the night in different parts of San Salvador. Once we left the bus, we barely saw each other!"

"If you had shown more respect for the nuns," Sister Consuelo said, "your fiancé would have respected you more, also. He would trust you more today, as your husband."

"That doesn't mean I deserve the way he's treating me." She listed some of the insults he had hurled at her, her anger holding her voice under control. "Eusebio knows this child is his! I'd never, ever — "

"I must ask you a very serious question. Amparo, did you ever, during your courtship with the man who became your husband, do anything that showed disrespect for him or yourself?"

"No, Sister Consuelo! A thousand times no! When we danced we were always out in the open where everyone could see us. We were fiancés for more than five years and we always behaved perfectly. He asked me to marry him when I was twenty and I didn't say yes until I was almost twenty-five because there were so many things I wanted to do in life before I had children. I preferred to wait. We barely kissed until we were married."

Sister Consuelo's cheeks turned red. "Remember that you are a teacher of innocent girls!"

"I'm trying to make things clear! I want you to see there's no reason — "

"When you married, why did your husband move to your village? Wouldn't it have made more sense for you to move to Antigua?"

Amparo hesitated, trapped by the cleverness of Sister Consuelo's eyes. "Yes . . . It's not common for a *ladino* to move to a Mayan village."

"Or for a man to move into his wife's house. A man provides for his family. If he is deprived of that pleasure, his self-respect suffers."

"No no no!" Amparo raked her half-closed hands across the top of the desk. "All that happened was that I remained friends with Raquel after I accepted Eusebio as my fiancé. After Sandra was born, Raquel took a great interest in her. She doesn't have children. Her husband . . . I don't know why she doesn't have children. But I used to go over there . . . Word of this spread in the village. Ezequial lives with his sister and her husband when he comes home. But he's hardly ever there. He works in Comalapa, in a house the Evangelicals run there."

"Did you see Ezequial at Raquel's house?"

"Only once! One time I dropped in and he was there. I came in the door with Sandra, and I could see how thin and hurt he looked seeing me with my daughter. He hasn't married. His bad leg makes him shy. I apologized to Raquel and left. I felt that every second I remained there was a knife-blow to his heart. But he wouldn't be happy if I'd married him. He thinks he would be, but it's not true."

"So you saw your ex-fiancé. And you are surprised that your husband is upset?"

"Only once! For two minutes! And Raquel and Sandra were there the whole time. But the village — you must know what they're like: people who have nothing better to do but spread untruths about others. They made it sound as though Ezequial was there every time. They even said Raquel wasn't there and I was alone with Ezequial!" She shook as she fought against tears. "I feel so alone. My husband doesn't trust me, I have to hide our arguments from my mother, my daughter is turning against me — "

"The mother is the centre of the family. As all others depend on her, she feels alone." Sister Consuelo paused. "Any path we choose involves loneliness. If you make your husband feel secure, he will have the strength to overcome what he knows in his heart to be falsehoods. Give him the opportunity to make that respect into a sign of his own strength. Yet, at the same time, be firm; by showing him respect, you will encourage him to respect you when you assure him of your loyalty."

Amparo sucked away her sobs, astonished at the same time by the nun's wisdom and her innocence. "Thank you, Sister Consuelo."

The nun got to her feet. "Let me get you a glass of water."

Amparo stood up to follow her to the kitchen. The sound of their steps echoed in the high-ceilinged vastness. What would she say to Eusebio when she got home?

NINE

THE EVENING OF HER MEETING with Sister Consuelo, Amparo returned home to find Eusebio alone. Inés had gone to her room. Mama had invited Sandra to eat dinner with her and Papa. This unspoken recognition that her marriage was in need of her parents' intervention made her furious. Sister Consuelo's counsel was swept away by rage. "And now you want to know why I am late? I suppose you think I was talking to Ezequial, who doesn't even live here? I suppose you are that stupid and suspicious?" The shock of each sentence thrilled and terrified her. It felt like the night when, buoyant from hours of dancing in the Pensativo stadium, she had accepted a sip from a bottle that a boy was passing around, half believing that the recipient contained water, and had swallowed the only shot of hard liquor of her life. "I'll tell you where I was! You won't be an *hombre*, you won't be *bien macho*, until I tell you, will you? You'll be happy to know that I was talking to a nun." She stepped towards Eusebio to confront his mute hostility. "I had to tell someone that my husband has accused me falsely and there's no one else I can talk to." Her voice broke and she began to sob harder than she had ever sobbed before. She felt her body stagger. Eusebio stepped forward and touched her shoulder. She pushed him away. Her power flooded back. "I'm not going to indulge you any more," she said. "You can think what you want, but you're not upsetting my daughter by sleeping on the couch.

We will sleep in the bedroom. We don't have to talk, we don't even have to touch, but we will be responsible parents."

She crossed the room to the toilet and closed the door behind her. As she looked at her face in the scuffed mirror, her first thought was that this was not the scene Sister Consuelo had envisaged. Her second thought was that Inés had overheard every word. Her third thought was that, without meaning to, Sister Consuelo had given her the courage to lose her temper.

Since that night they had been polite in front of others and silent when they were alone. Eusebio continued to regard her with a hard, wounded look. She had arranged with the Escuela San Fernando to continue teaching until the first week of her eighth month.

On the Sunday night prior to her last week of teaching, in the back room of the church, she opened the meeting of the Cakchiquel Women's Saving Club. Doña Soledad, the red plastic band of her wristwatch glistening beneath the cuff of her *huipil*, arrived late, excusing herself by saying her husband had brought her corn to peel.

"Our husbands must understand," Amparo said.

"*Ja!*" The women agreed, directing half-mocking frowns at Doña Soledad.

"*Konojel niqatij ixim!*" Amparo looked around the meeting room that the priest lent them. The women sat on cushions on the floor. Amparo, who occupied the largest cushion, faced the bare, whitewashed walls. The notebooks in which the accounts were written, and the envelopes containing the cash, lay in front of her. "We all like to eat corn! But we also like to come to our meeting." She went on: "The señora gringa cannot attend this month because she is working in El Quiché. We will start by passing the envelope and talking about our lives."

71

"Why don't you start?" Doña Soledad suggested. "How is your new baby?"

"I went to Doctor Asensio in Antigua last week, and he says my baby will be fine."

Doña Rosa, one of the village mothers, shook her head. "A faithful wife does not go to doctors. The only man who will see my body is my husband."

"The doctor is just doing his job, Doña Rosa," Amparo said. "When you pick up a chicken, you are not violating the rights of the rooster."

"I own the rooster!" Doña Rosa laughed. She displayed her six quetzales, placed them in the envelope and passed it to her neighbour, who showed her six quetzales, deposited them, and passed on the envelope.

Most of the women wore *huipiles* and traditional dress; the Evangelicals, such as Raquel, wore long skirts. Amparo, like the other younger Catholic women, usually attended the meeting in bluejeans and a blouse. Today, because of the late stage of her pregnancy, she was wearing a shapeless Evangelical-style dress. She had taken a long nap before the meeting and felt exhilarated by the reservoir of energy she had discovered on waking. "You do not notice that the chicken is naked, Doña Rosa," she said, "and the doctor does not notice that you are naked. Think of Doña Inocencia, who refused to go to the doctor. If she had been less ashamed, she might be at this meeting with us."

The speech put Amparo's Cakchiquel to the test. She was making mistakes, but the women understood her. She tried to conduct the meetings in Cakchiquel, particularly when the señora gringa was not present. The older women were self-conscious about their halting Spanish.

It had been difficult to persuade most of these women to join. She and Esperanza had spent hours arguing with them that they were not betraying their families by depositing six quetzales a month in a savings program. They had argued with them to keep their children in school, to discuss their health problems; in some cases, they had encouraged them to talk about their husbands.

"What else has been happening this month, Doña Rosa?"

Looking mortified, Doña Rosa stared at the floor. The other women urged her to say something. Pulling herself upright, the tiny woman said: "*Jeb'el ri job' niqa pa ruwi' ri juyu.* Good rain is falling over the mountains."

Doña Juana, another older woman who wore the village's *huipil*, nodded in agreement. "*Konojel taq che' yekikot.* All the trees are happy." Her bare feet were crossed in front of her. "My husband says the corn will be high this year."

"What else is happening?" Amparo asked.

Esperanza, seizing on the silence, said: "Thanks to the Peace Accords, the school will teach our children in Cakchiquel."

Doña Rosa shook her head. "*Nac . . . Re'n manäq ninjo jun tijob'äl pa qachab'al.* I don't want a school in our language. Why are the foreigners making fun of us like this? Why won't they let us become people like they are?"

"Doña Rosa," Esperanza said, before Amparo could open her mouth, "we are respecting our culture — "

Listening to her sister rehearsing the arguments they had used with Mama, Amparo felt her mind revolving around the word Doña Rosa had used to describe *ladinos*: foreigners, *käk winaq*. In the company of these women she could almost wrap herself in a shawl of pure Mayanness, like the three young Quiché women at the university. Perhaps, if she had not married a non-Maya, her life would be simpler. Yet it was a simplicity she didn't want: a Mayan man would be more possessive; she would have to fight to leave home to attend these meetings; she never could have stayed away for all the hours it had taken her to work with the señora gringa to found this club.

"Where's the envelope?" she said. "Has everyone put in their six quetzales? Do we agree that the Cakchiquel Women's Savings Club supports the government's plan to introduce schooling in our language in the village?"

Esperanza, Doña Soledad and most of the other younger women shouted, "¡Sí!", then rectified their affirmation to a loud Cakchiquel, "Ja!" They reached high above their heads to show their support. Doña Rosa and Doña Juana looked at each other, then lifted their hands. Only the Evangelical women did not raise their hands.

"We have a majority, but we do not have unanimity," Amparo said. "We can announce that by majority vote our club supports Mayan-language teaching in our school."

Raquel lifted her hand. She spoke in Spanish. "There are other women who wish to join our club. I wonder if we could discuss their cases . . . "

"You just want more Evangelicals here!" Doña Soledad said.

"The club should speak for all the women of the village," Raquel said, "not just for some."

She's been told to do this, Amparo thought. Not by Doña María, but by those gringo missionaries. She remembered the different ways in which Raquel had betrayed her over the years. Before she could open her mouth, Esperanza shouted in Spanish: "Some women are too brainwashed to speak for themselves!"

"*Re'n ix'ajpub'!*" Amparo said. "I'm the leader! I ask you to speak with respect. We must praise the heart of the sky and the heart of the earth to reach decisions that are wise." She continued to speak in Cakchiquel, sounding, she thought, like her mother taking control of her children. By restoring the

74

discussion to Cakchiquel, she brought in the older women, the mothers of their community; speaking in Cakchiquel reinforced her impartiality while it marginalized Raquel, who was uncomfortable in the language and would speak only in Spanish. "Our club is here for all, but to join you must meet two conditions. You must save six quetzales a month, and you must send your children to school. These conditions were established by the señora gringa and by the government. We cannot change them."

"But," Raquel said, "we must help women who aren't as free as we are. If we make too many rules people will be justified in asking whether it is really democracy we seek."

Raquel's words made the skin at the back of Amparo's neck go cold. The older women looked frightened. They remembered better than anyone how, during the war, the slandering of Catholic community organizations as outposts of Communism by the military and their Evangelical allies had been the prelude to disappearances and massacres.

" . . . We must be here for all women," Raquel was saying. "Especially the women who need us most. Christian humility, Christian charity, require us to make exceptions. Some women's husbands don't understand why it's important for children to go to school . . . " She looked around as others nodded in agreement. " . . . Some women's husbands are jealous or suspicious . . . "

Amparo felt the brush of Raquel's glance. "Enough!" The sharpness of her response startled them. "We all know the rules. If we admit women who do not send their children to school, the government audit office will withdraw our funding. We must follow the rules! Democracy is freedom, but first it is everybody obeying the rules."

She realized that in responding to Raquel she had spoken in Spanish. She bowed her head. "Where's the envelope?"

Esperanza handed it to her. Amparo displayed the envelope. "Here — we have each deposited our six quetzales. And here," she said, lifting up the larger, business-sized envelope at her knees, "is the envelope containing our savings to date. Now we will count the money."

Counting the money was an exacting, but essential, process. The women were anxious to see that the quetzales they had deposited in past months were still there, that the matching funds provided by the government had made their savings multiply. They wanted evidence that their neighbours had also put in their money, and that corruption had not siphoned off their investment. Each month, the señora gringa withdrew the envelope containing the money from the safety deposit box in the bank in Antigua; on Sunday she brought it to the village. This Friday Amparo had taken out the envelope and hidden it in the back of her refrigerator, wrapped in three plastic bags, until the meeting. She felt the cool damp manilla paper beneath her fingertips as she slid the larger envelope into position next to the smaller one.

She opened the smaller envelope and counted the money. "*Jun quetzal, ka'i' quetzal, oxi' quetzal* . . . " Counting in Cakchiquel forced her to concentrate. The base-twenty Mayan arithmetical system, which she'd heard Mama and Papa using at home, had never come as naturally to her as the base-ten system she had learned in school. She still hesitated when she reached the tenth woman's six-quetzal deposit and had to announce sixty as "three-twenty": "*Oxi' winäq.*" But she was determined to persist, if only to exclude Raquel, who had made her lose her temper.

"*Kajiwinäq junlajuj!*" she announced. Fifteen women, who had each deposited six quetzales, made ninety quetzales. She turned to the large envelope. At the end of each meeting those women who were literate wrote down the amount contained in this envelope.

"What is the amount in the large envelope?" Amparo asked.

"One thousand nine hundred twenty-three quetzales," the women repeated. Their faces displayed pride, happiness, even amazement that they had collected so much money. In the unimaginable United States of America, the señora gringa had said at the last meeting, this was almost three hundred dollars. Such power, she warned, brought the responsibility to adhere to democratic decision-making. Soon they would have to make choices about which institutions or business proposals they would support with micro-credit. They would have to manage disagreements, reconcile different points of view. The señora gringa had scanned the room with a meaningful look, as though only she suspected what lay in store for them. In fact, Amparo believed, it was the señora who was unsuspecting. It was clear to Amparo that the gringa did not recognize the seriousness of the rift between Catholics and Evangelicals. At the insistence of the government and the NGO, the Cakchiquel Women's Savings Club had absorbed Evangelicals who had been trained to hate the idea of community. Her clashes with Raquel during meetings were a whisper compared to the battles that would rage once they began to hand out money. She was determined to ensure that the organization not lose its way during this difficult stage. No one, not even her new baby, would pry her out of the leader's seat.

She opened the large envelope, took out the dirty quetzal notes, contained by rubber bands, unbound the first wad and started to count. The wad was made up of five-quetzal notes.

Her head bowed, she laid down the notes one by one: "*Wo'o, lajuj,wolajuj, juk'al* . . . Five, ten, fifteen, twenty . . . "

The other women stopped talking. This, too, was part of the ritual. Somewhere down the corridor, a door clacked shut, but otherwise the room was silent. Amparo continued counting.

"*Junwinäq junlajuj, Junwinäq junlajuj wo'o* . . . Thirty, thirty-five . . . "

Concentrating to avoid a mistake, she heard a flurry of quick steps, felt the sag of the floor beneath the cushions. Realizing someone had come into the room, she looked up.

A hand grabbed her hair, twisted her head up and pushed grinding hardness against her temple. Pain flashed down her back as she was wrenched upwards until the weight of her belly was tearing at her spine. Unwashed man-smell and the aftertaste of alcohol mingled with ground-in sweat and dirt. He pushed the barrel of the gun against her nerve-ends until the pain was unbearable. The women were whimpering. A hasty brush of movement. Out of the corner of her eye she saw Esperanza frozen halfway to her feet as a second man levelled his gun at her.

"Take the money, señor!" Amparo said. "Please. Just take the money!"

He cranked her head up and around. He had brown skin, soft black hair, high cheekbones, large white teeth, and dark eyes set slightly aslant. They could have been cousins. She felt the force of his desperation, his willingness to kill, like the thumping of blood in her own neck.

"We'll shoot you all and then take the money," the man who was holding Esperanza at gun-point said. The handkerchief tied around his face barely muffled his voice.

"Señor," Amparo whispered, appealing to the man holding her head. "We are all mothers. We have children to raise! In the name of God, señor — "

The man huffed as he tightened his grip. She felt lathered in sweat, ashamed of the mingling of his scent with hers.

"Maybe it's better if you don't raise your next child."

The masked man made a heel-dragging sideways step. He gestured with his gun at the two envelopes and the money piled on the floor. "Put the money in the big envelope," he told Esperanza. She stumbled forward. A wad broke open; wayward bills seesawed to the floor.

"*Hurry up!*" the man screamed. He repeated his jigging sideways step. Esperanza burst into tears. She clawed at the bills and pushed them into the envelope.

"Give it to me," the masked man said.

Her face lowered, Esperanza lifted the envelope. The man grabbed it.

The other man twisted the barrel of his gun against Amparo's temple like a gimlet. Her lungs beat in search of air like wind-whipped laundry on a line.

"Nobody leaves this room for thirty minutes," he said. "If you leave, we will come back and kill your children. You all have children and we know who you are — "

"Just take the money, señor." Amparo's tongue was thick in her mouth.

The man wearing the handkerchief limped out of the room with the money.

"Thirty minutes, or we kill your children," the other man said. He tightened his hold on Amparo, then threw her to the floor. The thud of the tiles froze her sweating cheek. She felt her child turn a somersault in her belly and she began to shiver.

TEN

MIST CONDENSED AROUND HER HEAD. She felt the child's twisting far down in her entrails as though it were marooned in a place beyond her reach. The Maker, the Modeller, Sovereign Plumed Serpent, wrought the world out of mist. Her mind strayed through the spaces beyond that haze when the mountains rose out of the water and the first people were fashioned out of corn and took the name *B'alam*. Her child was slipping away from her. Before she could reach through that space to pull the child back into the light which, inhabited by the first mother and the first father, would yield life, her strength abandoned her. As she floated on the waves that must recede before people of corn could take to the earth, a sharp smell penetrated her nostrils. *Pom.* Someone was burning incense. She heard voices: Eusebio's words derogatory, Mama's tones implacable in resistance. Amparo tried to reach out to them. She slipped away into the silence of the mist. She saw the people of mud who had preceded those of corn, deity's failed experiment in human life. The mud people's noses and eyebrows crumbled. People of wood, the heart of the sky's second failed experiment, who could not speak or worship their makers, stared without seeing her. As the people of wood drowned in the great flood, she slid farther down into darkness. The tendrils of incense prickling her nostrils were the lone thread leading back to the world. She saw four roads of different

80

colours crossing. Cold fear that she was already a corpse and this was Xibalbá, and the four crossing roads were the gate to the underworld. A chanting tapped through the walled-up silence. Nothing moved. She was blind, the cold rivetting her to the meeting point of the four coloured roads. The first four men, Jaguar Quitze, Jaguar Night, Jaguar Not Right Now, and Dark Jaguar, fathers of all subsequent lineages, hung before her eyes, then faded away. The tapping mingled with the tang of incense. The two sensations blended until they were a single interwoven fabric like the rope of terror that runs up a woman's spine when she fears for her child — yes, she had a child, and another one inside her — and in that instant her body swathed her in its aching weight and she was back in her room listening to the sound of the *curandera* chanting. The child turned in her belly, moving her body with its body, two bodies moving as one, as she and her husband had moved as one to make the child. The *curandera* must be Doña María's sister Eduviges, a woman simpler yet wiser than her sibling.

"*Raja q'o*'," she said. "She's here."

Eduviges stepped back from the side of the bed. Mama began to sing the song she sang when they were ill as children. She had sung these words over the beds of the children who had died in infancy, and over those who had returned from illness. Her voice was harsh but strong:

Kapae' wakami
Katz'uye wakami
Kapae roma utz qaw'a
Katz'uye wakami
(Stop here today
Sit down today
Stop here for our food is good
Sit down today)

Amparo, feeling the bulk of her hair beneath her on the pillow, whispered: "It's all right. I'm here."

"You've been away for two days."

At Mama's words, she remembered the man with the gun, the other thief's dragging gait. She lifted her hand, felt the bruise on her temple and began to cry.

"Stop crying," Mama said. "No one was hurt."

She passed from sleep to waking without lapsing into the mist. Every time she woke she felt sad. Eusebio entered the room and held her hand. Esperanza visited her and said: "In the next meeting we'll start saving again. I've spoken to the señora gringa and she says we cannot allow misfortunes to discourage us. The only solution is to start again."

The señora gringa had spoken to Esperanza, not to her. Her powers were ebbing. She had lost everyone's respect. Her child would be the offspring of rumour.

The day after emerging from the mist she sobbed until dusk. Esperanza came in for an hour but had to leave to look after her children. Eusebio and Mama poked their heads in the door. Mama told her that Sandra was staying with her.

That evening her contractions began. Eduviges returned, not as healer but as midwife.

Her son was born at the stroke of midnight, his body lodged across the line between one day and the next so that they were never certain which date to count as his birthday. From the moment she held him in her arms she could feel his timidity. He was afraid of life. Spirits had infected him with poisons in the womb. Her first thought was that his sickliness would make people think he was Ezequial's son. His nose and brows looked about to crumble like those of the people of mud. She held him against her breast, blinded by her need to protect him.

When Mama and Eduviges told her that Eusebio wanted to see the child, she whispered, "No . . . " But they had already left the bedroom. Eusebio came in the door. He was unshaven. She wondered if he was sleeping on the couch. He lifted the infant off her breasts, which had been untouched by his hands in months. She gasped. Eusebio raised the boy to head height and stared into his face. She could hear the child breathing in throaty gasps.

Eusebio started to cry.

"Don't hurt him!" she said. "Give him back to me!"

Eusebio was sobbing more loudly than a child. "He looks just like my grandfather!"

"He doesn't look like anyone yet," she said, finding the strength to sit up. She tried to pull the child away. "He looks like the people of mud. By tomorrow," she said, feeling herself growing calmer, "he will look like the people of wood. Later he will look like a human being made from corn. Then we can have him christened."

Eusebio gave the child back to her. He kissed her cheeks and her lips and her neck and her breasts. "I'm sorry, Amparo. Will you forgive me? I'm so sorry. I'm worthless, I don't deserve you. I promise I'll never treat you badly again. Amparo, please forgive me, can you ever forgive me?"

The words poured out of him as though they would never stop. She let him go on long after she had decided to accept his apology. His conversion was a miracle, and she knew that miracles must be savoured. At last, she lifted her hand to his cheek.

That night they slept together in the bed with the child between them. She woke in the morning to a loud knocking on the front door. When she reached the main room, the child slung across her shoulder, Esperanza was coming in the door.

Though exhausted from hours of feeding the child at short intervals, Amparo felt a great calmness ease through her at the boy's weight on her shoulder and the memory of her husband's sleeping body.

"Amparo," Esperanza said, "I'm going to have to bring Sandra back here — "

"Already? Can't you . . . ?"

"It's Yoli. She's run away with a gringo — "

"Run away? To Antigua?"

"She's going to be travelling with him as his girlfriend! Amparo, nothing like this has ever happened . . . I've never seen Papa and Mama so ashamed. Mama says she can never go to the market again. She's too humiliated to go to Mass."

"She has to go to Mass," Amparo said, struggling to absorb the news. "Maybe we can get her back before anything happens. We can go to Antigua — "

"You don't understand, Amparo. She's in the capital, at the airport. She's going back to his country with him."

"She's leaving Guatemala?" Amparo wrestled with her inert brain. "Leaving Guatemala?" They were speaking Spanish, but she said the word "Guatemala" in Cakchiquel: *Ixim Ulew*, Land of Corn. The idea of a girl travelling with a man she was not married to was horrible — but to leave Guatemala was beyond imagination. "What will it be like for her, Esperanza?"

Esperanza shook her head. Amparo felt the baby on her shoulder begin to cry. Trembling, she asked herself again what the world was like.

PART TWO

2003

ELEVEN

AFTER NEW YEAR THE FUEGO Volcano erupted every night. The village lost its electricity. "I'm afraid, Mama!" Pablito said as darkness fell. Sandra, assuming a lofty air, as though she spied womanhood winking at her from a nearby ridge, pretended not to hear him. When she came home from school she changed out of her uniform and into her favourite pink slacks. She moved around the house like a rich *dama* in a *telenovela*, brushing her hair, sliding a pink plastic hairband onto her head, staring in the bathroom mirror and asking if the two shades of pink matched. Amparo grew impatient with Sandra's apparent soundless dialogue with someone who wasn't there. In the dusk Mama closed the door of the compound behind her, and brought Amparo a portion of the black beans she had spent the afternoon cleaning. She set down the pail of beans in the doorway and looked at her granddaughter. "When your mother was your age she had been carrying Aunt Esperanza on her back for three years." As Sandra waltzed on, Mama said: "What a lucky girl you are to have nice clothes and not to have to work in the evenings."

"That's why we only have two children." Eusebio sat on the couch with his arm around his son. "We can give them things we couldn't afford if we had seven or eight."

"Why did you have so many children, Nana?"

Sandra's question took Amparo by surprise. At least her daughter was thinking about the choices a woman must make. The pink flush of the slacks accentuated the plushness of the girl's thighs. Next year she would start to menstruate. Mama had forbidden Amparo and Esperanza to eat eggs when they were menstruating, a practice she had continued with their younger sisters; in addition, she had watched their every move. Amparo planned to do the same with Sandra. Her daughter would not cause a repetition of the shame that Yolanda had brought on the family.

"When I got married, " Mama said, "it was the custom to have a child every year. A woman knew that her life was about suffering."

Sandra mulled this over. "I'm sorry, Nana." She stepped forward, hugged her grandmother, then uttered a formal excuse: *"Takuyu' numak."*

Amparo hugged her daughter and kissed her. Releasing her, she carried the beans to the counter and told Inés to set them to soak. Mama left; they ate before darkness closed in. In the absence of the television, Eusebio tried to distract Pablito by leafing through a magazine with him. They named the objects in each colour photograph until nightfall erased them. Pablito jumped to his feet and hugged Amparo's leg. "I'm afraid, Mama."

The walls of the valley deepened the night. The *maestras* at Escuela Tecún Umán told her that in Antigua the power had remained on most nights, but even when it had gone off they could open their shutters and see the distant orange of lava, high in the dark sky, sculpting the blackness as it spilled down the cone.

She put the children to bed with a candle. She and Eusebio retreated to their bedroom.

Even when the electricity was working, they undressed in the dark. They had acquired the habit as shy newlyweds. Amparo rolled under the sheets and slid her hand over Eusebio's hips to ascertain his nakedness. The miracle of shared nakedness dimmed the day's irritations, cancelled out her accumulated resentments: the way Eusebio doted on Pablito, his diffidence towards her siblings across the compound; the way, in a time that was even more remote from their present-day life, he had made false accusations. Now the thought of their nights together balanced the days they spent apart. Sometimes, in the middle of a difficult lesson, the weight of last night's embrace would overwhelm her with the reassurance that she was loved. The most private corner of her existence, which she could discuss with no one, had surged back with unexpected heat. Feeling Eusebio's weight at night, she fantasized about having a third child. The clasp of his hands on her curves, more womanly now than when she was a new bride, moulded this yearning inside her. She longed to give flesh to the fierce outcome of their reconciliation, their revived passion. She continued to spend precious money on condoms for Eusebio, purchased in a pharmacy where no one knew her in the village of San Felipe, on the edge of Antigua. Only when she thought of the world beyond her bedroom did she pause. If she ignored her own advice as a woman of thirty-six she would be unable to face the young girls she had recruited into the Savings Club in the wake of Yolanda's flight. She gave the girls lessons on health, education, self-respect, and the importance of having no more than two children and raising them responsibly. As she had grown older, she had become aware of the influence of her example. When she smothered her moans in Eusebio's collar bone and dug her fingertips into his shoulder blades, confident that no child would emerge from this coupling, the community's judgment weighed on her.

Eusebio lay on his back in the darkness. The sting of his sweat filled Amparo's nostrils and tingled in her pores as the cool night air settled over their bodies. He ran his hand down her side in a parting trailing-away of passion that yielded to their falling-asleep trickle of conversation.

"That boy I told you about who came into the shelter last week . . . He's gone. The boy in the next cot says he went to *El Norte*. The boy who left invited the other one to go with him but the second boy was afraid."

"He's right to be afraid. Imagine what'll happen to him, trying to sneak into Mexico by himself then over to the other side, all without a *coyote*."

"That's what worries me. That he's willing to try. The shelter used to get people coming down from the highlands. They got stuck here on their way to the capital. Now a lot of the people who end up on the street were born right around Antigua. Their families don't look after them. But we're getting fewer from the highlands because they're all going north . . . What kind of country do we live in, Amparo, that so many people want to leave?"

"You see why I try to promote my culture? If young people value their traditions — "

"But if they can't eat . . . "

"Yes, people must eat. But when times are hard being secure in your culture gives you strength. Look at Raquel. I thought she would go to north after Jorge left her. Her aunt in Arizona could have paid for a *coyote*. I was sure she would go! And she stayed. She stayed because she rediscovered her culture."

"But Raquel is a person with a house, with means."

"She has a house. She barely has an income." Amparo felt soothed that they could talk about Raquel without the spectre of Ezequial intruding. She took his hand and laid it on her side.

"I'm worried about my job, Amparo." He snuggled closer to her. "The contract is up for renewal again. I don't know if the gringos will pay for another five years. Last time Guatemala was a country coming out of a civil war, a country everybody wanted to make into a democracy. Since September 11th they've forgotten about us. Señor Robinson says that when he talks to Washington everything is about the Arabs . . . "

"But our problems are getting worse."

He took her in his arms. She lay against his broad, accommodating body. As he shifted his weight to secure his grip, his flaccid penis gave her thigh an amiable nudge. The sealed-up darkness felt thrilling. "I'm just warning you," he said.

"We'll get by. I've got my job at the language school. We have our house, we have our children."

"We're lucky Sister Consuelo recommended you to Tecún Umán."

"Yes! She told Don Teófilo that I was a good teacher and he should hire me." She stared into the blackness, giving free rein to her doubts. "If only it were more reliable! Look at the last few months — all Don Teófilo was able to offer me was one student who stayed in Antigua for two weeks. A lot of the maestras didn't work at all during the five months before Christmas. We couldn't live without your job."

They slid apart and lay side by side. "So," Eusebio said, "if — "

"For the moment we'll be fine. These Canadians have just arrived and after that there are gringo students and some people from the American government. Don Teófilo says there'll be more tourists again soon. The gringos won't stay at home forever." Feeling herself grow tired, she said: "Tomorrow morning we have a meeting. The manager is going to talk to us about the students. Then I'm going to go see Yoli — "

"Amparo — "

"I have to try to bring the family together."

"Why is it always you? With so many brothers and sisters . . . "

"I feel bad for Mama and Papa. They're so ashamed. They refused to mention Yoli's name the whole time she was away."

"She's married now. There's no more scandal. And they say she and her gringo live in a mansion. If you can call him a gringo . . . "

"He's a kind of gringo. He came here to do the gringos' work during the war." Amparo pulled the blanket up to her chin. "I'm still angry with Yoli. Getting what she wanted meant more than respecting her family . . . But she's my sister! And nobody's set foot in her house. And when she comes here, Mama and Papa just look at the ground"

Eusebio wrapped his arm around her. " . . . Amparo . . . always trying to make things better . . . "

They fell asleep. In the morning Amparo woke sneezing and pulled on her nightgown. She hurried to get Sandra ready for the minibus that she and other parents funded to take their children to school in Antigua. Pablito, who was attending the village school until they found the money to send both children to private schools in Antigua, dragged his feet.

"I don't like school, Mama. I want to stay here with you."

"You can't stay here with me because I'm going to Antigua to work."

"I don't like the way the teacher looks at me when he's drunk. The other kids make fun of me."

"Nobody makes fun of you. You're a boy like all the others. When I was a girl I had to go to school barefoot. Everybody laughed at me but that didn't stop me from learning."

"I'm afraid!"

"Sometimes I think you're afraid of life!"

"Amparo," Eusebio said, in a warning tone.

They stared at each other. She bristled at the tensing of his jaw, the dull simplicity of his eyes, as though he were innocent of responsibility for her anger. At the table, Inés, thin-waisted in her Quiché *uq*, was placing Sandra's toast and *frijoles* in front of her. Pablito began to cry. Amparo turned away, her fury defeated by protectiveness. As she hugged her son, tenderness towards Eusebio ebbed back. By the time they left the house half an hour later, she felt drained. The minibus had honked outside the compound and picked up Sandra; Inés was walking Pablito to school. She and Eusebio sat side by side on the Bluebird bus down the mountain. They held hands and did not speak. When they arrived, they made their way out of the market, crossed the Calzada and went their separate ways through the cobblestoned streets.

Unlike most of the language schools in Antigua, Escuela Tecún Umán was not arranged around a courtyard. The small tables across which students and instructors faced each other from eight to twelve every morning, and sometimes again in the afternoon, were indoors. Squeezed between a secondary school and the walled-in ruins of a gigantic church that had crumbled in the 1773 earthquake, the sprawling old house did not offer the familiar sensation of faceless adobe walls relaxing into the ample proportions of a sunstruck courtyard or garden; this experience was so familiar that she remained perpetually surprised by Escuela Tecún Umán's lack of access to the heavens. A government administrative building that had fallen into disuse before becoming the Antigua home of the coffee-growing family who had sold it to Don Teófilo, the school had a high-ceilinged entrance hall from which a spiral staircase revolved to the second floor. Two large ground-floor rooms had been filled with wooden tables and chairs. Don Teófilo and his sons had offices at the back of the ground floor.

The front room was full when she arrived. The Canadians must be bringing a lot of students for Don Teófilo to have called in so many *maestras*. She did not recognize some of these young women. Don Teófilo stood against the wall wearing his white shirt and V-necked dark blue sweater beneath a black jacket.

A throat cleared. The *maestras* turned their heads. She realized that her arrival had interrupted the *canadiense* manager, a trim, compact man, who was standing at the head of the room. His small blue eyes transmitted displeasure. She wished she could speak English to apologize. As she looked around in search of an empty seat, she found she had no alternative but to meet his unyielding stare. His voice swooped towards her in supple, educated Spanish without the usual comical accent. "Before you entered the room, señora, I was saying that Antigua is not a large town and so there is no excuse for either students or *maestras* to be late for classes. I hope you agree?"

"I agree, but I don't live in Antigua. It takes me longer to get here because I live in a village." She could not believe she was uttering these words; Don Teófilo might fire her for such insolence. But the man's stare provoked her.

"You think that's a good excuse for being late?" the manager said. "Which village do you live in?"

Offended — what would the name of her village mean to this *käk winaq*? — she noted the other *maestras*' scrutiny. Searching for an empty seat, she muttered her village's name.

"Ah," he said. "You must know Doña María."

"Yes, señor, I know Doña María."

"Please send her my regards. Tell her Ricardo remembers her. As I was saying . . . "

She turned her face into a mask, praising the heart of the sky and the heart of the earth for enabling her to hold back her tears. Don Teófilo was pointing her towards a chair at the front of the room. She dreaded what he would say to her when this was over.

The manager said that each *maestra* would receive a textbook corresponding to the level of the student she would be teaching. She must follow the textbook thoroughly — *ideteni-damente!*, he said, repeating the word — to ensure that she completed the assigned chapters during the month of January. This was vital because the students were receiving credit for their courses; if they did not complete the relevant chapters they would be unable to continue their studies when they returned home. So completing these chapters was more important for them than learning to talk? Most gringo clients, such as the Christian universities from the United States, simply wanted their students to be able to speak Spanish to go into the villages and flip people upside down. That was what the tourists wanted, also: to be able to ask directions and order meals and bargain in markets; they didn't care about textbooks. Amparo didn't dare ask the question; no other *maestra* asked it either. They would all bow their heads and nod, then go on to teach as they had always taught, engaging the student in conversation. Amparo felt her irritation growing with this man and his insistence that they all waste their time at his meeting.

" . . . It is indispensable," he said, "that you teach the textbooks rather than criticizing them. You may find that the books contain some colloquial expressions or structures with which you're not familiar. This doesn't mean that the Spanish in the book is wrong. It simply means that, in addition to exemplifying the Spanish you speak, the book exemplifies the Spanish spoken in other countries, such as Spain and Argentina . . . "

Indispensable, colloquial, exemplify . . . Most of these girls wouldn't understand those words. If Don Ricardo knew Guatemala well enough to be acquainted with Doña María, he should be aware that teachers had little education. Amparo understood him only because Don Julio had made her read novels. As his fine phrases unfurled, her anger returned.

When he finished they applauded him. His tight face sagged into a smile as he sidled over to exchange a few words with Don Teófilo. Amparo, relieved to see the *jefe* occupied with this client, decided to escape. When she reached the door of the room, Luisa Méndez, who had been teaching at Escuela Tecún Umán for more than a decade, was talking to Nancy Robelo, a curvaceous young girl in tight bluejeans who had streaked her hair blonde, a style she was able to get away with because her skin was a soft medium-brown, lighter than that of the other *maestras*, or even, although it would be scandalous to voice such a thought, that of Don Teófilo. Unlike some of the other *maestras*, Nancy did not pretend to be more than she was.

"How boring!" Nancy said. "None of the other foreigners make us listen to them like that."

"He thinks he's important because he's bringing a lot of students," Amparo said.

Luisa Méndez lifted her finger. "We had Canadians when I started teaching here. They don't even believe in God — "

"But they're Protestants," Amparo said, "like the ones from the United States?"

"They don't talk about God, like you or me or the Yanquis," Luisa Méndez said, shaking her head. "But they want to make the world better."

"A better world without God?" Amparo looked past Luisa's wagging finger. Don Teófilo was clapping the manager on the shoulder. She, in turn, touched Luisa, then Nancy, on the elbow. "I have to go. My sister's waiting for me. My sister who's married to a gringo who runs a security company . . . I'll see you on Monday."

She walked out of the room without looking around. If Don Teófilo wished to fire her, he could phone her. She wasn't going to be humiliated in public. But, *ay Dios*, let him forgive her! What if he actually fired her? And if Eusebio's Señor Robinson couldn't get his contract renewed, and if they had no work . . . ? She shouldn't have responded to the manager with such disrespect. This Sunday the first sin in her confession would be pride.

TWELVE

THERE WAS NO EASY ROUTE to Yolanda's house. It was not in a village but in a field outside Antigua where the mayor had given one of his cronies a concession to build houses outside the boundaries of any village. A place that lacked a history to the point where its women did not know which design to embroider on their *huipiles*. Amparo followed a narrow cobbled street towards the edge of Antigua. She could not imagine living in a place that did not have a *huipil*.

Trucks ground past, forcing her to step into the mounds of garbage rotting on the roadside. Gaunt dogs cast her wary, whimpering looks. Bitter smoke from a peasant's fire of immature branches stung the air. She came around a corner and saw the wire mesh fence corralling the dozen two-storey stucco houses with red-tiled roofs, set down like enormous booths for watchmen among tall yellow grass. She entered the lot with a wave at a bored security guard and looked for the house whose number Yolanda had given her.

A small grandmotherly woman wearing a Santa María *huipil* answered the door. When Amparo, using Spanish in deference to her surroundings, asked for Yolanda, the woman called: "Señora! There's someone to see you."

Yoli swept into the room wearing a gold-trimmed black dress falling to just below her knees. Her shoulder-length hair curled up at the ends. Amparo's head buzzed as she struggled to accept that the *ch'i'p*, the youngest of the family, was this great lady. "How are you, Amparo? And Eusebio? And my little Sandra and Pablito?"

She did not ask about Mama and Papa. She led Amparo through large rooms with big windows that let in the light through fine-meshed grates. One upstairs room contained a computer, a printer and a fax machine. Next door was the bedroom — Amparo felt heat in her face at the sight of the double bed — and across the hall were two empty rooms. "You have plenty of room for your children," Amparo said as they descended the stairs.

Yoli's hand fell on her arm. "Oh, Amparo, I don't know if I'm going to have children."

"How can you not have children? Everybody has children!" When Yoli had run away, Mama and Papa were terrified that she was pregnant; now that she was twenty-three and married, it was her childlessness that was a scandal.

Yoli tugged Amparo closer as they sat down on the living room couch. Two glasses of Coca-Cola awaited them on a bronze tray. "David is fifty-one. He was married in his own country when he was nineteen. His daughters are almost thirty. He's already a grandfather. I don't think he wants more children."

"You don't *think*? Why don't you ask him? Ask him, for heaven's sake! Explain that in Guatemala every woman must have children!" As she peered into Yoli's face, her awareness that her little sister would always be younger and more beautiful than she, retreated before her observation of a tightness of cheek, a wariness in the eyes, that reminded her of Yoli's years in a faraway country that appeared on television as a war zone.

Yoli stroked her cheek as though caressing a private hoard of knowledge. Amparo caught her wrist. "What was it like, Yoli? What were you doing over there?"

"David was sent here as a *consejero* . . . " Completing Yoli's phrase in her head, Amparo thought: not any adviser, but a military adviser. But *militar* was the word neither of them could utter. " . . . After a few years, he resigned from his post at home. He had a pension and he liked Guatemala. He put his money into a friend's business. They designed products for national defence here in Guatemala, then in Central America."

"Weapons for the army."

"Not just weapons!"

Amparo said nothing. She had promised to heal the rift, not wrench it wider.

"It's business," Yoli said in a curt voice in which Amparo heard a perfect imitation of her husband.

They looked at each other with evasive stares. Amparo remembered the postcards: Yoli's only communication during her absence, except for her two phone calls, the first to announce that she had married, the second, three years later, to tell them that she was returning to Guatemala. The alphabet on the postcards' stamps looked like stretched ears of corn. Amparo had always felt stronger when she learned about other worlds than when she rejected them; yet her resolve faltered. She told herself the war was over. Yet the dead were still dead, five hundred villages had been razed, the culture that had existed before the war could never return, Mayan traditions had continued to fray rather than reviving as Don Julio had said might happen once the fighting stopped. It all, somehow, seemed to be Yoli's fault. If her sister had conceded some awareness of events, Amparo would have found forgiveness easier. But the anger would not go away. She flung her arms around Yoli as though she wanted to squeeze the breath out of her. Rolling her back against the couch until their heads nodded close enough to one another that their identical strands of long dark hair fell together, she whispered in Yoli's ear: "What were you doing all those years?"

To her astonishment, Yolanda sobbed. She emitted an abrupt sighing moan. "My big sister," she said. She gave Amparo a kiss on the cheek. A half-ashamed smile crossed her face. "Don't worry, Amparo. It was a good life."

"Where were you living?"

"I was living in a beautiful place. David started a club. There was a swimming pool with a view of the sea. I woke up every morning to palm trees and sunlight. I could eat in the restaurant; I didn't have to cook unless I wanted to. I could lie next to the swimming pool and listen to music. In the evening I put on my *huipil* — "

"Do women wear *huipiles* in his country?"

"Only in David's club. He called it The Mayan Riviera. On the wall behind the bar there was a photograph of the Agua Volcano. ¡*Qué preciosa*! It was almost more beautiful than the real thing. There were weavings and those paintings of Lake Atitlán that they sell to tourists. The cook made *frijoles* and chicken with avocado. In the evening there was music, sometimes rock-and-roll, sometimes typical Guatemalan music. The Ixil women would sing — "

"There were Ixil women? There on the other side of the world?"

"David worked in the Ixil," Yoli said. Amparo slid across the couch, laying her hand on her sister's leg. "He found these orphan girls in a model village. They barely spoke Spanish. He thought I could speak to them, but Ixil's so different from

Cakchiquel that I couldn't understand anything. He decided to give these girls a better life."

"A better life? He took girls whose families had been killed in the war, who had been forced into a concentration camp, and carried them away to the other side of the world?"

"You should've seen their apartments, Amparo! And the food they ate! Important men came to this club. Army officers who were fighting the terrorists, businessmen — "

"The girls were prostitutes!" Amparo got to her feet and looked down at her sister. "You turned *traje* into a uniform for prostitutes! Is that what you did to our traditions? *Anchi jat jech'ël?*" She was shaking too hard to move.

"Quiet, Amparo. The servant'll hear you."

"Let her hear! She needs to know that she's working for a man who kidnaps orphaned Mayan girls and turns them into *putas!*" Amparo got to her feet and shouted: "¡Señorita!" When the servant woman failed to appear, she shouted: "*Ke taq re'!* Over here!"

The servant appeared in the doorway, hunched inside her *huipil*. Her face shuddered as Amparo spoke to her in Cakchiquel: had the mistress' sister in a gringo house ever spoken to a servant in a Mayan language? The poor woman wouldn't know whether the greater offence lay in responding in the language or in failing to respond.

"Our parents were right to be ashamed," Amparo said in Cakchiquel, her frustration at her ailing vocabulary compounding her fury. "You were one of them, weren't you?"

"Never . . . I was the boss's wife. David's daughters and I, we were off limits. David's older daughter, Duchi, married one of the officers, but she did it properly, with a betrothal and a wedding . . . "

"Unlike you, a shameless girl who ran away — !"

"Amparo, did you come to my house to insult me?"

In the doorway, the servant looked past them without seeing them.

Amparo struggled to breathe. "You were a madam in a brothel and you expect not to be insulted? If Mama and Papa find out — "

"You think too much about Mama and Papa."

"You're talking about your parents, Yoli! Where is your respe–?"

"Amparo, you've spent your whole life in that compound and you've never grown up."

For a moment Amparo was too startled to reply. "Who are you to say I haven't grown up? You don't even have children. You're still a little girl. It's only when you become a mother and have responsibilities that you understand the debt you owe your parents."

Yoli turned away. She must be lonely sitting in this house all day. In spite of herself, Amparo felt ready to forgive her sister. Her head filled with visions of Mayan prostitutes in Ixil *huipiles* parading around a swimming pool with the sea crashing behind them.

She sat down on the couch and sipped her Coca-Cola.

"I'm sorry," Yoli said. "I'm not the kind of sister you wanted, am I?"

"I want you to be happy. Who did you talk to all that time?"

"To David's daughters. They were suspicious of me at first, but by the end we were like sisters. At first I could only talk to David because no one else spoke Spanish. Then he hired a bodyguard who'd also worked in Guatemala. I learned English from television and songs, and talking to the men — I spoke to David's daughters in English. I didn't learn their language — it's too hard — but my English is really good now."

"Yoli! You could get a job in a tourist agency or a hotel — "
Seeing Yoli smile in an almost condescending way, as though it
were she who was young or naive, Amparo said: "You shouldn't
have gone away."

"That's not fair." Yoli's tone was calm. "Nobody says that
about Rafael."

"That's different. Rafael had a proper courtship. He got
engaged to his gringa, then he got married."

Four years ago a brother who was a year older than Amparo
had helped a blonde gringa with a backpack, who was lost on
the streets of Antigua, to find the language school that was
arranging her accommodation. Megan, a psychologist from
Phoenix, Arizona, had taken a six-month leave of absence to
learn Spanish, the language of many of her patients. By the
end of her stay in Antigua, she and Rafael were engaged. It
made things easier that Megan was Catholic. They married in
the village church and again in Phoenix, where they now lived
with their baby son. "We all miss Rafael, but he behaved like a
gentleman."

"He didn't always behave like a gentleman! He used to go to
bars in San Felipe. Nobody cares what men do!"

"It's up to women to make men care," she said. "Does David
come home late?"

"Not usually. Sometimes he spends the night in the capital."
Yoli shrugged her shoulders. "It's business." She gave an idle
stretch, riding the flex of her leg to her feet, and asked the
servant to clear away the glasses.

The old woman from Santa María stood in the doorway,
watching them with a concentration that Amparo found
unnerving.

She observed Yoli's supple lines, the body that cried out to
give birth. A rich woman could have as many children as she

wished . . . Her sister was rich! "Life is hard here," she said. "Eusebio and I could be starving tomorrow. My job depends on gringo tourists coming to Antigua and his job depends on a gringo NGO. It didn't use to be like that, not even during the war. The *ladinos* would steal our land and starve us and kill us, but our survival depended on us, not on foreigners." She hesitated. "I think I may have lost my job this morning." She told Yoli how she had interrupted the manager.

"You think you know better than anybody. I remember how you used to tell me what to do." Yoli took a quick step that was almost a petulant stamping of her foot. "Maybe you *will* lose your job."

Amparo got to her feet. "I wish I could do a divination." She looked at a shawl hanging on the wall. On a shelf above the television there was a photograph of a childlike Yoli and a vigorous dark-haired David standing before a tree with a crooked trunk. Photographs of two light-skinned young women with dark hair and hooded eyes followed, then a photograph of a staring toddler. Next to the photographs stood a golden candelabra. She stepped past Yoli, skirted the television and lifted the elaborate candlestick off the shelf. "We could use this . . . It wouldn't be as reliable as with a *curandera* or a daykeeper, but it would make me feel better. Please, Yoli . . . " She heard her voice rise. At what point had Yoli become the dispenser of benefits and she the beggar?

"We can't, Amparo. I don't have any incense." She flashed her most provocative smile. "Why would I have incense?"

Amparo turned towards the kitchen. "¡Señorita!" she shouted to the servant. "*Q'o pom?* Is there incense?"

"*Ja.* I have incense," the servant said, entering the room. She hesitated. "I have coral seeds and crystals, too." Her Santa

María-accented Cakchiquel, clogged with extra syllables that sounded like pompous flourishes, made Amparo smile.

"I need a divination. But I don't know the Mayan calendar." She heard her voice catch. "If only our parents taught us better!"

"Señora," the servant murmured. "My father was a daykeeper. I'm not initiated, but . . . "

"Amparo! You can't! Not here."

"Why not? We're in *Ixim Ulew*, no? We're in our country, we can follow our customs."

Yoli sat down on the couch. She whispered: "Doña Manuela came to us when she married a soldier in a unit David was advising."

"Those Santa María women! They can't resist soldiers."

Doña Manuela came into the room holding a small cloth bag. They hesitated. The most convenient place to perform the divination would be on the table in front of the couch. But servants did not sit on the couches they dusted. Manuela set the bag down on the television. As the three of them crowded together, Amparo felt the differences between them, imposed by foreigners, peel away. The older woman opened the cloth bag and spread the seeds and crystals across the plastic top of the television's casing, avoiding the ventilation grille at the back.

"We need candles." Amparo picked up the candlestick.

Yoli caught her wrist. "We can't use that. It's from my husband's religion."

"We're using it for a religious ceremony." She looked at the eight-branched candlestick with the holder which, Yoli explained, as though this made clear why they shouldn't use it, held a candle with which one lit other candles. The candlestick glimmered between them in the large-windowed brightness of the living room, its branches swarming like the limbs of a golden squid beached on the sand at Monterrico. Amparo set the candlestick down on the television. "Your husband's candlestick is in Guatemala now, so it's going to become a little bit Mayan."

Doña Manuela went to the kitchen and returned with candles and matches. She set candles in two of the central stems of the candleholder and lighted them. She stuffed two more holders with incense, which she set alight. Grey-white tendrils rose into the air; their odour lifted Amparo out of herself, like a childhood experience recaptured.

Doña Manuela spoke in Cakchiquel, invoking Ixmucane and Xpiyacoc, and thanking Tohil, the god of fire, for providing flame for the candles. She closed her eyes; her mouth grew pinched. She emptied the contents of the bag onto the top of the television. The seeds and crystals made a rattling sound. Amparo remembered that she must place coins — the fee for the ceremony — on the empty bag. She found three quetzales in her pocket and laid them on the cloth. Manuela continued to murmur as she mixed the seeds, invoking Hurricane, the bringer of rains, who destroyed the world at the end of each cycle of human existence and provided the fertility for life to begin again. Manuela's right hand rotated over the bundle of seeds. "We thank the sheet lightning and the rain, we borrow from the lord of the damp mists, the lord of the breezes, the lord of the mountains. We borrow their knowledge of the weather of the future . . . "

The servant hunched forward. Her hand struck with jaguar-like quickness, seizing a fistful of seeds. Yoli shuddered. With her left hand, Manuela brushed aside the remaining seeds and crystals. She distributed the seeds in her right palm over the top of the television in lots of four in parallel rows, then counted the days of the calendar. She was reciting neither the old Long Count calendar used for historical dates, nor the lunar calendar of 360 days plus five days of peril, but rather the 260-day ceremonial calendar divided into thirteen weeks of twenty days each. The names of the days rang against her ear. Doña Manuela counted one day for each lot of seeds. Amparo inhaled the sweet incense.

"*Ahau, Imix, Ik, Akbal, Kan* . . . " The servant, now invested with the presence of gods, paused to murmur: "At her legs, her arms. At her legs, her arms . . . " The strength of the lords of the weather filtered into Amparo's arms and legs. "At her legs, her arms . . . "

Amparo had never stood more firmly on her feet.

Doña Manuela reached the last lot of seeds, bowed her head and gave thanks to the lords of the weather who had lent her their foresight and their knowledge of time to give her this glimpse into the future. Continuing to stare into the pattern of seeds, she said: "The augury is complete. The first news is good. The wind blows over the mountains, the sky is clear." Her clotted Santa María pronunciation made her announcement sound both portentous and absurd. "You will keep your job."

Amparo did not rejoice. She sensed that the news was not simple.

"Beyond this time in which you have work, the weather is full of storms. Your life will be marred by dangers, the path forward is not clear and may not be lengthy. You will endure these trials and find the path which is yours only with help from your family."

. . . *may not be lengthy* . . . What would happen to Sandra and Pablito without her? As she bowed her head and shuddered, a ferocious embrace pinned her. For the first time in ten years, Yoli was hugging her like a sister.

THIRTEEN

NEXT MORNING, AS PABLITO WAS moaning that he was too sick to go to school, the phone rang. "Amparo? Teófilo Contreras here . . . Amparo, the *canadiense* manager — "

She looked at Sandra and Pablo: they would need new clothes before the rains came. "Please forgive me, Don Teófilo! It was a mistake. I'm so ashamed — "

"Are you willing to teach him? He wants to learn Cakchiquel."

"Oh, no, Don Teófilo, it's very difficult to teach Cakchiquel!"

"The *doctor* insists. Amparo, you're my only *maestra* who can teach Cakchiquel."

"As you wish, Don Teófilo. Thank you very much for the work."

"What a stubborn woman!" Eusebio said when she put down the receiver. "You're afraid he'll fire you, then he offers you work and you tell him you don't want it."

She scowled, but it was no use: they were laughing at her. She hugged her daughter and her husband. She ruffled Pablito's hair. For these three people she would do any work in the world.

On Monday morning she arrived at Escuela Tecún Umán twenty minutes before classes started at 8:00 AM. She was surprised by how relieved she felt to see the Canadian girls — there were only four boys — milling around at the foot of the winding staircase. It appeared that Don Teófilo might be right: the tourists would return to Antigua and they would all have work. She kept her ebullient mood hidden as she sat down opposite the manager. It was important, especially when teaching gringo men, to begin on a formal footing.

"My name is Amparo Ajuix de Hernández," she said, stressing the married woman's *de*, "and I apologize for interrupting your talk."

"Don't worry," he said, opening a notebook in front of him. He responded to her name by mentioning that he, too, was married. His wife had stayed at home in Canada where she had a busy career. He shook his head, as though resuming his focus on Guatemala. "Did you give my regards to Doña María?"

The fixed stare of his small blue eyes unnerved her. "How do you know Doña María?"

"I've worked in Guatemala before, with refugees. A group that fled to the Pacific Coast during the war — "

"Did they end up living on the side of a volcano?"

"Yes," he said. "Those people. Somebody suggested your village might help, and sent me to talk to Doña María." He laughed. "I have to say that she was quite unhelpful."

She leaned closer. The manager was like the men who used to come into El Tesoro.

She recited the introduction she had prepared, explaining to him that she did not speak Cakchiquel perfectly, and that this was one of the problems the language faced. "Our parents were ashamed of this language and didn't teach it to us very well. I can teach you the Cakchiquel of my village, but in other villages they speak differently. And in my village most of the young people speak to each other in Spanish; only about thirty percent of us speak Cakchiquel perfectly." She hesitated. "It's very difficult to learn Cakchiquel, and you can't talk to very many people in it. You must know this before you begin."

"These are exactly the problems that interest me."

Condemned to work harder than her colleagues, she bent her head. But her feeling of resignation was pricked by an upsurge of emotion. She was talking to somebody who, like Don Julio, could feed her need to understand. During the first two hours of the class, she made him write the letter corresponding to each of the thirty-two sounds of the Cakchiquel alphabet. She showed him how the x had a shushing sound that didn't exist in Spanish. Anticipating the mistakes that foreigners made, she illustrated the difference between qäk, "red," and käk, "foreign," explaining that he must pronounce the q far back in the throat. She told him to listen to how a tiny pause could turn a sound into a separate letter, making k utterly different from k'. At ten o'clock the break came. The Canadian professor, a small Asian woman who was being taught by Luisa Méndez, came downstairs from the private room where she had her class, and she and Don Ricardo went out onto the street to talk. Vendors crowded around the door, offering the students tortillas spread with avocado paste. Amparo walked to the bottom of the staircase, where the maestras exchanged impressions of their students. "How's the professor?" she asked Luisa.

"Simpática," Luisa said, "but these Canadians aren't normal gringos. The professor is a chinita. Imagine!"

"Yes," a younger woman echoed, "and my student is hindú." She shrugged her shoulders with a hapless expression. "My gringa is darker than me!"

"Mine is a real gringo," Nancy Robelo said with a toss of her head that made her highlights ripple. "He even has blue eyes. He was in the army!"

"¡Un militar!" the first young woman said with a down-turned mouth.

"He's not *bruto* like a Guatemalan soldier," Nancy said. "He worked for peace . . . to keep peace . . . in . . . ex-Yu-go-e-slav-i-aa." She smiled as she extracted the word from her mouth like a length of corded rope.

"Maybe you'll marry him," Amparo said.

"Amparo! I'm not from Santa María!"

As the younger *maestras* giggled, Luisa, her eyes narrowing, said: "Amparo, why did Don Teófilo give you the manager to teach?"

"How do I know? He phoned me and asked if I'd do it."

Luisa observed her in silence. Uncomfortable with her scrutiny, Amparo turned away.

After the break they reviewed pronunciation. She felt relieved at how perfectly she possessed these sounds. She spoke Cakchiquel better than she had given herself credit for; being with Ricardo made her feel more Mayan. She obliged him to repeat and repeat. He was better at vowels, having difficulty with consonants like *b'*.

"*B'ey*," she said. "Road."

"Bay," he repeated.

"*B'aq*," she said. "Bone."

"Back," he repeated.

"*B'alam*," she said. "Jaguar."

"Ballam," he said. He looked up. "Let's keep working on that one. I'd like to be able to say 'jaguar.'"

"*B'alam*." She made him repeat the word fifteen times. His face turned almost blue as he strangled his breath to produce the required hiatus. He asked her questions she didn't understand: was this *b* aspire-something or glotta-something? The students at the nearby tables paused in their lessons as he repeated, "Ballam, ballaam, baallaam . . . " She was struck by this manager's lack of fear of appearing ridiculous in front

111

of young people half his age who were under his authority. It was impossible to imagine Don Teófilo allowing himself to be corrected in front of his *maestras*.

"Let's try something else," she said, when his repetitions had petered out.

"What's the word for one of those little woven bags you buy in the markets?" he asked.

"*Ya'l,*" she said.

With a sheepish smile, he risked a short sentence: "*Q'o jun ya'l.* There is a bag."

Noon was approaching; she was worried about Pablito's cold. She taught Ricardo to say "'Till tomorrow!" — *Chuwak inchik!* — gathered her books and stood up. As Ricardo got to his feet, Don Teófilo came over to shake his hand. Luisa Méndez, descending the stairs in conversation with her little Chinese woman, conceded Amparo a circumspect nod.

Amparo walked to the market and rode the bus back up the mountain to the village. When she reached the house Mama was in the kitchen. "Pablito came home," she said. "The bad spirits have got into him."

"He just doesn't like school."

"He's vomited twice." Mama followed her towards the bedroom. "His vomit was smooth and yellow. That means the spirits got in through his eyes."

Setting down her Cakchiquel-Spanish dictionary, Amparo regarded her son's form huddled under the covers. Pablito's face was hot, his skin dry; there was a yellowish fleck in the corner of his mouth. "How are you, *mijito?*"

"Mama." He struggled to sit up. Coughing seized him. He coughed until his tongue stuck out of his mouth. He began to gurgle. Mama came to her side with a bowl.

Pablito vomited into the bowl. The vomit was yellower than corn, as though the matter out of which the boy was formed had been extracted in a bright gruel. Amparo could not believe that the substance that filled the bowl was coming from Pablito's tiny stomach. The boy collapsed back into the sheets and began to cough, driving the fetid backwash of his vomiting into their faces. Amparo ran for a damp cloth to clean his mouth. Mama carried the bowl to the bathroom. "That's the third bowl he's filled in two hours," she whispered. "That's what happens when the spirits get in through their eyes."

"We have to get him to Antigua. The hospital — "

"The hospital can do nothing about this."

Amparo hesitated, torn between respect for her mother and fear for her son's health. "Should I get Doña Eduviges?"

"Doña Eduviges is old. Now the best *curandera* is your friend Raquel."

"All right." Amparo walked out of the house, crossed the yard and clanged the iron door of the compound behind her. She hurried down the street, as though set upon by the blank stucco walls. The boy in the bed filled her mind. She felt the nearness of her own death, the fragility of life in a world that had been created and destroyed many times, the need to bequeath descendants to the cycle of life and death in order to live on as an ancestor. The dearness of Pablito's soft flesh made her stumble. As she turned into the square, her mind filled with a vision of the four coloured roads that crossed before the gate of Xibalbá. The four colours — black, white, green, and red — covered the door of Raquel's house in horizontal bars; the purple that had been painted over was barely discernible beneath their fresh brightness.

Raquel answered the door wearing her *huipil*. Her hair slid on her shoulders in two tightly woven braids. "*Sakar*, Amparo," she said. "*La utz a'wech?*"

"*Matiox, matiox.* But Pablito's ill. You've got to come. Mama says spirits have entered him."

Raquel stepped back to usher her in. A poster over the sink displayed the symbols and names of the twenty days of the week in the ceremonial calendar. Tangy, pungent incense permeated the house. Raquel went into a back room and emerged carrying a lumpy woven bag.

After Jorge had come home for the last time and beaten her, Raquel's thin, beautiful, haunted features had swollen up until they muffled the shape of her bones. She had gone to her preacher, to the gringo missionaries; then, dissatisfied with their answers, she stopped talking to these people. When she disappeared from the village, everyone assumed her aunt had paid a *coyote* to take her to Arizona. On her return, months later, she revealed that she had been studying with a Mayan priest in Santa Cruz del Quiché. She went to villages in the hills around Antigua and spent weeks speaking with the women there, praying and performing ceremonies, until she recovered her Cakchiquel and her traditional knowledge. Amparo felt a reproach in Raquel's convert's grip on the Mayanness that she herself slid in and out of from hour to hour. It pained her that Ezequial no longer returned from Comalapa, his religious disagreements with his sister having become irreconcilable.

They crossed the compound, ignoring Esperanza's youngest daughter, who was playing in the dust. Amparo led Raquel inside. Raquel greeted Mama respectfully, addressing her as "*ixoq.*" Before approaching Pablito, she lighted incense on his bedside table and prayed to the heart of the sky and the heart of the earth. Raquel picked up the incense and waved it in

114

Pablito's face until smoke wafted into his nostrils, making him cough.

His coughing turned into a hoarse dredging sound. At the point where his lungs seemed to have been scraped raw, he leaned forward. Mama returned with her bowl. Mealy yellow vomit poured out of Pablito until the bowl was half full. Amparo feared for his ability to draw breath, but as the final dribbles fell from his lips, he collapsed onto the pillow with a loud, rank-smelling wheeze that reassured her that he was still alive. She ran for a fresh damp cloth to clean his face. Mama, gesturing with the slurping bowl, said to Raquel: "That's the fourth time today."

"It can't continue," Amparo said. "His stomach's empty."

"It will continue." Raquel looked taller in her thinness. "It will continue until we expel the spirits. We need a pixcoy bird."

Before Amparo could object, Mama said: "Doña Eduviges will sell me one." Amparo wanted to take her son to the clinic. Yet she was wary of defying the other women's certainty. She went for her purse and handed Mama two folded ten-quetzal notes. She piled coins on the bedside table in indication of her ability to pay Raquel's fee. Mama left the house. Raquel sat down to await her return as the room filled with incense and her son shuddered in his sleep.

Amparo pulled her chair closer and laid her hand on Pablito's head. She felt the heat turning his thick hair as dry as tinder. Raquel looked her in the eyes. "Yellow vomit is a women's illness. It affects young girls near the time of their moon, particularly those who have just become women. It's caused by not eating enough garlic. Or by eating eggs when they shouldn't. That's what allows the spirits to get in through their eyes."

"You're telling me Pablito has a girl's illness?"

"This is a sign." She leaned forward. "Amparo, your son may be a mother-father, *jun chuchqajaw*. If he is, you must let me train him."

Amparo shook her head. "That's not for him."

She had spoken in Spanish. Raquel replied in the same language: "And what is your world, Amparo?"

"My world is my family." She glanced at her sleeping son. "Things are good between Eusebio and me now."

"Even though you are sitting across from a gringo four hours a day? You know what they say about those schools: the *maestras* fall in love with their students."

"They may fall in love with them, but the sensible ones don't do anything about it. The gringo goes back to his country, but the *maestra* must stay here."

"Your sister Yolanda is married to a foreigner."

"Yes, and look how that hurt my parents." Her anger at Raquel for having lured her into this conversation ebbed. Against her will, she responded with a smile to Raquel's sympathy. "You're right. It's hard not to fall a little bit in love with them when you're talking to them for four hours a day. I'm teaching a manager; the manager for the Canadian semesters in Guatemala. He speaks Spanish, but he wants to learn Cakchiquel. He's not a very warm person, but he's courteous and he's interested in our culture." Something in this sentence made her uncomfortable. "Personally, I think it's very useful to teach in a school. If a woman knows herself, it can stabilize her marriage. You can develop friendships with other men in a formal situation where you know nothing will happen. You can have your fantasies, but you are a *maestra* doing a job. The important thing is to have your fantasies and not to act on them."

"I think," Raquel said, "that you will always be a Catholic." After a moment, she added: "It's fine for the woman to have her fantasies then come home to her husband, but men aren't like that. Their fantasies become real only when they act on them. That's what I learned with Jorge."

"I'm sorry you're alone, Raquel."

"I'm happier being alone. I used to cry so much when he didn't come home! But now he's living in the capital, probably with another woman, and I'm unable to remarry because I'm still legally married."

Amparo looked at the boy in the bed. "I'm sorry if I said anything hurtful."

"I'm starting to think," Raquel said, "that women must not be afraid to act on their fantasies."

"Don't say that! What a lack of respect."

"A lack of respect to whom? To Jorge, who betrayed me? To Doña María and the villlage gossips? These people deserve respect and I don't? Even our ancestors, *ri qati't qamama' Kaqchiquel,* allowed women to get divorced in certain circumstances."

As cowed by Raquel's cultural mastery as by her anger, Amparo bowed her head. "A married woman must be careful."

Raquel lifted Amparo's hand from Pablito's head and took her palm in hers. "You've learned that lesson well, haven't you?"

They sat holding hands, listening to Pablito's wheezing sleep, until Mama returned. She carried a hemp bag that wriggled and squeaked.

Releasing Amparo's hand, Raquel bent over the bed with hands clasped, calling upon the heart of the sky and the heart of the earth, the two who unify into one while remaining two and hence incarnate the world, which is both unity and distinctness. Her words enhanced her presence in a way that seemed to draw her thin body upright. Pablito coughed in his sleep. "I've seen this before. When the vomit is yellow" — Raquel even used the Cakchiquel word for yellow, *k'aän*, when nearly everybody used Spanish words for colours — "like the yolk of an egg it will continue for at least three days after the stomach is empty. We must ask the spirits to leave."

She pored over Pablito's face as though it were a sacred text. She cajoled the spirits, assuring them of her respect but insisting that it was time for them to move on. Her words, buoyed up by the thick whitish incense, rode around the room like tiny boats. "The blockage is at the level of his chest," she said. "You won't get food into his body until this is gone."

Amparo felt hemmed in by the other two women. Mama passed the hemp bag across the front of their bodies. Raquel reached into the bag and extracted the still, trembling bird, trussed rigid by the expert lock of her long fingers. "You must open his mouth."

Amparo lifted her hands towards the bird's tight-clasped beak.

"Not the bird's mouth! Your son's mouth!"

To her horror, Mama was laughing. "The bird will eat the spirits," she said. She reached forward and gave Pablito's shoulder a rough shake.

Pablito's eyes opened. He coughed and coughed, tried to sit up and fell on his side. "Mama! Nana!" he said. "What's she doing with that bird?"

"She's going to make you better, *mi amor*. Open your mouth." She tried to cover her lack of conviction with urgency. Yolanda's maid's divination had felt as irrefutable as the June rains, yet she couldn't believe that this bird would cure her son's vomiting. Was she Maya, or wasn't she? Raquel, whom she still wasn't used to seeing in a *huipil*, claimed that any middle ground was betrayal, yet she couldn't help how she felt. She couldn't help wincing as Mama held Pablito's jaw open, hauling his coughs into frightened whimpers, and Raquel, chanting, moved the bird in a slow arc towards his lips. As the bird's head plunged between Pablito's bared teeth, Raquel loosened her grasp. The bird's beak cranked open, its upper and lower mandibles wedging against the upper and lower rows of Pablito's tiny baby teeth. Boy and bird were fixed together, two faces becoming one. In its panic, the pixcoy bird opened its beak wider, lodging itself more irrevocably in the boy's mouth as Pablito bit down in fear. Amparo saw their throats branch into one another like spliced lengths of pipe. Pablito's coughs stuttered to a halt. His body arched in the bed, his craning head thrusting the bird's tailfeathers into the air like a warrior's trophy. She turned her eyes away, unable to avoid thinking of the movements of Eusebio's body during love.

Pablito's neck stretched, his head flung back in silence. The pixcoy bird was gulping.

"The bird is swallowing the spirits," Mama said.

Raquel leaned forward, murmuring under her breath. The rising sequence of gulps that filled the pixcoy bird's stomach drowned out her words.

Raquel's hands swooped, unlatching the pixcoy bird from the boy's mouth. She clamped the bird's beak shut, swayed it through the smoke three times, then left the house. She returned with her hands free.

Pablito slept. Amparo pulled the sheets up to his shoulders.

"Your son is cured," Raquel announced, her thin face gleaming. "Cured because a woman wasn't afraid to act on her fantasies."

FOURTEEN

NEXT MORNING, WHEN SHE WALKED into the broad front hall, Amparo heard Luisa Méndez, addressing Ricardo as "Mr. Manager," ask him about his Spanish course. Devious Luisa, always checking up on other teachers so that she could pass on gossip to Don Teófilo.

"But I'm not studying Spanish," Ricardo said in his loud, too-clear voice, "I'm learning Cakchiquel."

"Amparo can teach Cakchiquel?" Luisa mulled this over. "*Amparo es indígena* . . . I didn't know that Amparo was an Indian." Lifting her chin, she said: "These are dialects. My parents spoke a dialect, but I was fortunate to learn the Spanish language so I am not an *india* as they were."

"They're not dialects," Ricardo protested, with a directness that made her stand straight-backed and upright, even as it terrified her. "The Mayan languages are languages, just as Spanish is a language. Some of those languages have local variants, which are dialects . . . but a language is not a dialect just because it's spoken by indigenous people!"

Luisa, her head held high, accompanied the Canadian *profesora* up the curving staircase to the second floor. Amparo slipped into the main classroom, where each *maestra* sat across a small desk from her student. She opened her books in front of her before Ricardo could realize that she had overheard the conversation.

"*Sakar, Amparo,*" he said as he sat down. "*La utz a'wech?*"

"*Utz matiox, Ricardo. Y ret?*"

"*Utz matiox.*"

"*Matiox ri.*"

They smiled. The creases around his eyes and mouth made her realize that his whiteness had led her to underestimate his age. Her respect for him increased. This was a man who had been coming to Guatemala for many years; he would know important people here, people to whom she would never gain access.

His homework had been to write sentences using the vocabulary they had learned yesterday. He lifted a hard-backed notebook and read the sentences in a voice that was more nervous than she had expected. "*Re'n q'o jun ya'l q'iak. Q'o jun b'alam pa ri nuya'l.* I have a red bag. There is a jaguar on my bag."

She corrected his pronunciation of *b'alam,* stressing the *b'* again. He repeated the sound. She folded her hands together on the table beneath the ruffled white cuffs of her blouse. In muted Spanish — they lowered their voices when they spoke Spanish — she said: "You don't really have a bag with a jaguar on it?"

"I had one. I gave it to a friend."

Una amiga. He had told her he was married. Rushing on to avoid revealing her disappointment or being roped into his moral lapses, if those were what he was on the verge of confessing to her, she whispered: "Is it a woven bag? The background is red and the jaguar is white?"

"Yes." He stared at her. She had caught his attention, driving away thoughts of his *amiga.*

"And the jaguar is walking?"

"Yes . . ."

"You bought this bag in my village? At our market?"

"No. In Mexico. Two years ago, when I was in Chiapas."
The sounds of students repeating Spanish phrases echoed off
the wooden classroom floor. She sensed his attention beginning
to wander.

"I make those bags," she said. "I weave them, I sell them in
the market in our village. I'm the only person who makes bags
like that. The bag you bought in Chiapas was made by me."

She saw him struggling to absorb her words. "How can you
be sure?"

"A few years ago I was invited to go to Chiapas and Oaxaca
to sell my weaving and work with the Mayan women there, but
I couldn't afford the bribes you have to pay to get a passport,
and the Mexicans wouldn't have given me a visa anyway, so
a gentleman here in Antigua, a very kind gentleman who
has since passed on, arranged for my weaving to be sent to
Chiapas." His washed-out blue eyes followed her. She had his
attention again. "Later, when he paid me for the bags that he
said had been sold there, I almost refused the money because I
thought it was charity. I was left with strange feelings towards
him. But now, with what you've told me, I see he was telling the
truth. It makes me remember him with great tenderness."

She had noticed Don Julio's cough the last time she had
seen him, but had thought nothing of it. Later she heard that
he had died and that his family had hired a lawyer to prevent
his young wife from inheriting El Tesoro. The man who ran
the restaurant now, who had bought it from Don Julio's cousin,
had reduced the size of the bookstore. Sonia, the widow, had
left Antigua.

His voice low, Ricardo asked: "Would you like to travel to
other countries to sell your weaving?"

She shook her head. "It's not possible. My brother, who's
married to a gringa, tried to arrange for me to go to Arizona

for two weeks, but, even if I could afford the passport, the American Embassy doesn't give visas to people like me . . . For us, even going to Mexico is a dream."

"But there are lots of Guatemalans in the United States, no?"

"*Ladinos* from rich families that can pay bribes for passports . . . Or they're illegal. Or they went as refugees during the war — but many of those are also illegal. I have a friend from my village who went to California." She lowered her voice. "*¡Él es ilegal!*"

To her surprise, Ricardo shook his head. "No. People are not illegal." He seemed almost angry. "They can be *indocumentados* . . . There are people who have documents and people who don't have documents. But no human being is illegal."

She had never thought about it like this. Were there other people in those countries who thought as Ricardo did? That you could be just as worthy and dignified living in another country without the proper papers as at home, in the village where everyone knew you?

Troubled by these thoughts, she shook her head. "I could never do that. I obey the law. Even if that was the only way to travel, I could never turn myself into a criminal."

Don Teófilo passed through the room, ringing the bell that signalled it was time for a break. Ricardo got up and joined the students in the doorway to buy a tortilla spread with avocado. Avoiding Luisa Méndez, Amparo spoke with Nancy Robelo, telling her about Don Ricardo's bag. Nancy told her about all the countries where her soldier had worked as a peacekeeper. They were boasting about the men they were teaching as teenaged girls might champion the boys in their class on whom they had crushes.

After the break, Amparo taught Ricardo the verb *ibinik*, to walk. "*Re'n ibi'n, ret abi'n, raja nibi'n . . . .*" They practised this verb, recounting the places that different people walked to, then returned to the previous day's vocabulary. He still couldn't pronounce the *b'*, but he was starting to distinguish *a'* from *ä*. Now she could tell when he was saying *a'q*, pig, and when he was speaking about *äk*, chicken.

During the second half of the class she felt restless. As the final minutes approached, she folded her hands across her Cakchiquel-Spanish dictionary. "You really bought one of my bags in Mexico? Oh, I wish I could see it just to know it's true!"

"If I hadn't given it to my friend, I'd be happy to show it to you. Of course I can't be sure it was your bag . . . "

"Ricardo! Come to my village. I'll show you our market and the compound where I live."

"With great pleasure," he said, after a moment's hesitation. She had the impression that working so far away from his wife had made him withdrawn. A man needed a wife, even a foreign man whose emotions were less strong than those of a Latin American. "I haven't been to your village since I went to talk to Doña María . . . I'm sure it's changed a lot." Punctual as always, he closed his notebook.

"Yes," she said, gripped by an unexpected nervousness. "You can bring a couple of the students with you."

"Of course," he said, observing her.

She met his eyes. Worried that the invitation to visit her village had been an excessive intimacy, she allowed her gaze to wander to a flurry of movement near the front door. The little Chinese professor who taught the Canadian girls politics and economics was coming in the door, a huge smile on her face. She was escorting a tall man whose black polo neck shirt stretched over a body subsiding into a middle-aged spread. He had light brown skin, yet the ghost of high Mayan cheekbones lent his face a dashing, dramatic appearance accentuated by the clipped grooming of his moustache. His eyes, set behind spectacles with the finest of gold frames, were large, dark, impervious to others' scrutiny.

The world had changed the day she had seen this man on television.

She seized Ricardo's arm. Her voice crushed into a whisper, she said: "That's Comandante Vladimir! He was with the guerrillas!"

Ricardo turned around in his seat. Vladimir stopped and acknowledged him with a brief handshake. Comandante Vladimir knew her student! "He's going to be teaching a course for us on the politics of the civil war," Ricardo said, getting to his feet. "Don't leave, Amparo. I'll introduce you to him."

FIFTEEN

P ABLITO, WRAPPED IN THE RABBIT GOD blanket, sat in front of the television. Without stopping to put down her books, Amparo kissed him on the forehead.

"*Utz*," Mama said. "He's fine. Just quiet. *Mem ri a akua'l.* Your child is mute."

"He's pretending to be tired because he doesn't want to go to school tomorrow." Sandra stood in the middle of the room, a skipping rope dangling from her hand, her pointy pre-breasts darting the front of her pink child's blouse.

"Your brother was ill. You should thank God that he has recovered." Setting down her dictionary and notebook on the kitchen table, Amparo walked towards the alcove, where Inés, her hair in tight, shiny braids, was paring chicken for supper. She longed to tell someone that she had shaken hands with Comandante Vladimir. Her student, Don Ricardo, knew him! But references to the civil war gave Mama the shivers. Amparo told Sandra to help Inés. In a low voice, she asked Mama: "Why isn't Inés in the market?"

"I couldn't look after Pablito and cook supper at the same time. When Sandra came home I sent her to get the girl."

"And why isn't Sandra cooking? She's going to be a woman. She must learn to cook. We buy her good clothes, we pay for her to go to school in Antigua — "

126

The door opened. "Papa!" Sandra shouted, running across the tiles. Pablito wriggled in his nana's arms.

Eusebio gave Sandra a distracted hug. He looked shackled, as though his weight had slid down into his ankles and feet. Amparo stepped forward. "Leave Papa in peace, Sandra. He worked hard today."

Sandra retreated with a dramatic scowl. Amparo looked her husband in the eyes. "We have to talk," he murmured.

"Where are you going?" Sandra asked. "I want to watch the *telenovela* with Papa!" Amparo thought of all that her daughter would never understand because she had not walked into a schoolroom barefoot. If Amparo had given birth to a baby every year, as Mama had done, Sandra would be a responsible girl who looked after her younger siblings. When she had closed the door, she threw her arms around her husband, nuzzling his chest.

"I met Comandante Vladimir today!" she said, when she broke out of his embrace, "He looked very handsome, like a film actor, but hard, even though he's heavier now. It made me realize how hard those men in the *guerrilla* were. Don Ricardo had a meeting with him! He's hiring him to teach a course to the students."

Eusebio looked at her. "Amparo, my job is over."

In the stifling silence, he went on: "The office in Washington did not renew Señor Robinson's money."

"But they can't — the young people need shelter. They can't close the drop-in centre."

"From now on, young gringos will work in the drop-in centre for free. They don't need the money; they can do it to have a different experience. They call it volunteering." He shrugged his shoulders. She saw that he was repeating words spoken

127

by Señor Robinson: words that made little sense to him. The uncertainty in his eyes filled her with pain.

"They can't take away your job!" She flung herself against his chest. "They can't!"

"But if the gringos work for free . . . "

She tugged on his neck. "How much longer — ?"

"Till the end of the week."

"That's all?"

"Amparo, there's no money . . . "

"But can't Señor Robinson — ?"

He shook his head. His helplessness made her impatient and angry. She couldn't let her impatience show for fear of crushing him. Once again, her marriage was going to depend on her quashing her feelings. She fell against him and tightened her arms around his ribs until he gasped.

The children knew better than to ask questions during supper. She had instilled at least this much respect in them. In the morning, as Inés left for the market, she wondered how long they would be able to afford her. Each time she allowed this thought to enter her head, she cancelled it out by assuring herself that Eusebio would find another job. But which job? He could go into a Korean *maquila*, work twelve-hour days in a pounding din and spend most of his meagre wage on bus fares to come home for eight hours out of twenty-four. There was no work in the village, and, with the decline in tourism, very little in Antigua. She, too, might soon be unemployed. A handful of the Canadian students would sign on for extra hours once their month of intensive language training had ended, and Don Teófilo had a few contracts with gringo organizations and religious universities that would carry Escuela Tecún Umán through the months of February and March, but they could easily be laid off at the end of March. She wilted at the thought of months without an income. In the sleepless nights, when she and Eusebio exchanged inconclusive murmurs, her mind returned to Doña Manuela's divination: *Beyond this time in which you have work, the weather is full of storms. Your life will be marred by dangers, the path forward is not clear and may not be lengthy. You will endure these trials and find the path which is yours only with help from your family.*

The help she received from her family would be meaningless unless she could provide them with security. If the path ahead of her was not lengthy, she must ensure her children's security. The path she found, for as long as it might last, must be the right one. Nothing else mattered. They would breathe her into eternity as an ancestor. The thought of leaving Sandra and Pablito unprotected made her frantic. She had done all that a woman could do: she had educated herself beyond anyone's expectations; she had worked for Don Julio, she had become a teacher; she had founded a savings cooperative; she had run her weaving stall. She had tried every means available to improve her life and those of her neighbours. She had ransacked the resources of Antigua, where money and opportunities were more plentiful than elsewhere in the country, and still she was sliding backwards. When she gazed out the window, riding the bus down the mountainside, she saw a landscape of desolation spread below her.

She must do something extraordinary.

On the Saturday morning after his last day of work, Eusebio refused to get out of bed. His lethargy filled her with energy. "You can't spend the whole day there," she said. "We have to make life better for our children!" She lifted her *traje* off the hook in the cupboard. Once she was dressed in her Mayan skirt, *huipil,* and headband, she grabbed her pillow and slugged him over the head with it. He lay as quiet as a chicken whose neck had been wrung.

"You can't spend the rest of your life in bed!" As she closed the bedroom door behind her, the sunlight reflecting off the tiles of the vacant living room enveloped her in air, space and possibility. She felt like the hero twins, Hunahpu and Xbalanque, emerging from Xibalbá, survivors of a ball game in the underworld. She felt as Blood Moon must have felt after giving birth to these two errant heroes. Her own children, already fed breakfast by Inés, were playing with their cousins in the yard of the compound. Rage and energy tore at her stomach in a memory of the tearing that had brought Sandra and Pablito into the world. She rummaged in the closet until she found her bundles of thread. She mst make something new. Outside, her brother Fernando and his Mam wife were hoeing the tiny garden they cultivated in the dust in front of their house. "I'm going to the market," Amparo said to her children, making a point of speaking in Cakchiquel. "When your father wakes up, tell him he can find me there."

She reached the market to find Inés hoisting aloft woven bags and embroidered shirts on a long pole to set them in the spots where they hung on display. A thirst for work, pure work, raced through her. Even though it was Saturday, few tourists were likely to be bused up from Antigua. She crossed the market and bought a jar of *atol de maíz*. Pulling out her favourite workstool, she sat down, opened the bundles, and dipped the threads in the *atol*. A quick dip was all it took: corn, from which the first people had been made, also nourished her fabrics. The threads clustered up like worms. She stretched them out, spacing them evenly on the smooth concrete. She lifted the rack-like loom out of the back of the stall and, shooing the servant girl aside, set it up in front.

The morning rushed past to the rhythm of the dipping of her *charq'oy* pole and string. She lifted and pulled, lifted and pulled. Her mind became concentrated and free of worry. The thread on the sixteen-pole loom grew into a red ribbon, then a narrow band. Inés sat hunched in the stall, watching her in a way that made Amparo wonder whether the girl was remembering her mother weaving. Mama had taught her to weave; she had helped to teach her sisters, from Esperanza, who was a year younger, all the way down to Yolanda. She must give Sandra proper lessons soon, before she began to think of herself as too good for weaving. A woman who could weave might be poor, but she would never starve and never be unable to clothe her family. Amparo was aware that these words were less true than they had once been, yet such certitudes comforted her.

As lunch approached, the red band on her loom broadened. She probed the weft with her fingers. A black skirt sheathing a pair of slender legs approached. "Look at this," Raquel said, waving a copy of *Prensa Libre* containing a story about government corruption. If Raquel had a family, she wouldn't waste her energy on problems nobody could solve.

"Keep your voice down," she said. Talking about politics had flipped their conversation into Spanish. The village's mayor belonged to President Portillo's political party, the FDR. Raquel continued in an angry whisper: Portillo was a drunken young lout, a puppet of the Evangelical General Ríos Montt, who had unleashed fifteen months of scorched earth warfare on the highlands in the 1980s. Amparo remained silent as Raquel denounced the general, remembering how, as an Evangelical, she used to defend him. She said in Cakchiquel: "Many of our people see Portillo and Ríos Montt as their lords who protect them."

"But this understanding is false!"

"You took a long time to change your view. Others may take longer."

Inés brought Amparo a plate wrapped in a plastic bag. She could feel the warmth of the tortillas against her palm. Next to the tortillas were *frijoles*, a splash of avocado and two slender strips of white breast meat. Raquel excused herself as Amparo began to eat.

"A bus!" Inés said. Her thin hands clasped.

Amparo's first thought was not for the tourists but for Inés. She was aware of the forced solicitousness with which she had been talking to the girl since last night. The hardship that was about to descend on the family would affect Inés first. Her contribution was minimal, her position ambiguous; if she wished to remain during hard times, she would have to earn her keep. The girl gave a slight bow, as though stressing the usefulness of the information she had just provided. Amparo finished her last tortilla. The girl slid the plate and cutlery into the plastic bag, knotted it, and put it away at the back of the stall.

Amparo resumed weaving. Her energy flowed back, filling her with the urge to create. She knew, also, that the sight of a woman in traditional Mayan dress weaving was an excellent way to attract tourists. She bent her head as she spotted a gangly middle-aged gringo with broad shoulders.

The gringo approached with a lilting stride. He was huge, even allowing for the fact that she was sitting on the floor; his crisp bluejeans went on forever. He said nothing, observing her weaving. His receding hair had turned a pasty colour between blond and white. She broke her rhythm to nod towards the stall. "*Pase adelante, señor.* Please go ahead, sir."

He did not move. His plain face and simple eyes unnerved her, as gringos' faces often did: she expected people with money to be craftier.

"Go ahead, señor. The girl will show you the weaving."

"*Utz a ruk'u'x ri ken*," the big gringo said. "*Inkux x'on . . . ?*"

Amparo didn't hear the rest of his sentence. She felt flooded with shame. The voice continued to flow as though it were coming from the gringo's mouth, which was impossible because this voice was spinning out Cakchiquel expressions that even Mama would struggle to formulate. Amparo didn't know what *ruk'u'x ri ken* meant until the gringo's broad, pale hand signalled the central rod of her backstrap loom. *Díos mío, que vergüenza*: he knew the Cakchiquel technical terms for every part of the loom! With a few exceptions, such as *charq'oy*, Amparo used the Spanish words.

His effortless Cakchiquel poured over her bowed head. He dropped down into a crouch, observing her over his bent knees. "*Disculpe, señora. ¿Usted habla Cakchiquel?* Do you speak Cakchiquel?"

He became a tourist again. His Spanish, far more than his Cakchiquel, had a strong gringo accent. "Where did you learn all those words?" she asked him in Spanish, aware of the sob in her voice. Conscious of the crowd that had gathered around them, she kept her eyes focused on her loom.

In his loud gringo Spanish, the man said: "My name's Willard J. Franklin. I belong to the Kansas City Kakchiquel Club. We're a bunch of ordinary folks who get together twice a week to practise Cakchiquel. We come down here once a year to tune up. We call ourselves the KCKC. We spell Cakchiquel with a K because it makes our name go down smoother."

"Pleased to meet you," Amparo said. Feeling that if she was really a person who believed in promoting her culture she must risk exposing her Cakchiquel in public, she beat down her shame long enough to ask him: "Where did you learn all those words in our language?"

"We learn a different vocabulary every year," he said, his native pronunciation of *choltz'ib'*, "vocabulary," erasing his identity as a tourist. "This year we learned weaving vocabulary."

Amparo stared at the concrete. In the crowd's silence, she heard Inés shuffle her feet. She had forgotten that this man was a potential customer: shame abolished all other emotions.

Polished black shoes stepped forward beneath a black Mayan skirt. A self-confident voice addressed Willard J. Franklin in Cakchiquel that was more assertive for having been relearned in adulthood. "My friend is very humble. She does not tell you that she weaves beautiful bags. Her bags have a jaguar that walks. No one else in our village weaves bags like these."

"*Q'o jun ya'l,*" Amparo said, looking up at Raquel. "There's one bag."

Her head bent, she lifted and pulled, lifted and pulled, extending the red fabric. The long bluejeaned legs and the slender black skirt went past her shoulder. The clacking of the loom competed with the sound of the gringo's murmured negotiations with Raquel. The sound of the large gringo speaking Cakchiquel held the crowd mesmerized. She saw Doña María pressing forward, her slender daughter and six-year-old granddaughter at her side. She hoped Doña María felt remorse: she, who had helped to sabotage the adoption of her language by the village primary school, should take this gringo's mastery as a sign of how wrong she had been.

Defiance brought Amparo to her feet. She brushed down her skirt as she stood up. Turning around, she found Willard J. Franklin testing the weft of her red bag between his thick pale fingers. "*Utz*," he said, pronouncing his judgment. He asked a technical question in his supernatural weaving vocabulary.

Raquel's thin face flushed with a heightened sensitivity. "I do little weaving myself," she said.

Aware of the crowd at her back, Amparo provided a lengthy response in vigorous Cakchiquel. She related how weaving techniques had been passed down through the generations by the women in her family. He seemed pleased by her response and gave her a good price for the bag: not the foolish overpayment of an ignorant tourist, but the calculated compliment of a gentleman. She opened her mouth to thank him. Before she could invite him to look at her other weaving, he had turned to Raquel. "You say you do little weaving. What is your work?"

"I'm a *curandera*," Raquel said.

A huff of derision from the crowd. Amparo knew without looking who was responsible.

"I'm very interested in Mayan medicine," the gringo said. "Last year the KCKC studied Cakchiquel medical vocabulary."

Raquel slipped out from between the high walls of the stall with a nimble movement that drew the gringo along in her wake. They skirted the crowd and walked down the back passage of the market in avid conversation, the gringo's resounding voice showcasing his knowledge of the vocabulary of traditional medicine. Amparo approached the remaining tourists and invited them to visit her stall. She offered to show her loom to a middle-aged woman in a straw hat. The prospect of Amparo cornering all the sales sent the other women back to their stalls.

The woman in the straw hat, also a member of the KCKC, if less fluent than Willard J. Franklin, bought a wallhanging that Mama had woven. It was Amparo's last sale of the day. The tourists drifted around the market for another hour. Amparo was about to return to her loom when a car horn sounded. It sounded again, in a quick double burst, then a third time. Amparo followed Inés to the front of the market. The cream-coloured minibus with "TURISMO" on the side was full and idling. The impatient driver honked again. Large, crusted-looking gringo faces turned to stare as Willard J. Franklin crossed the square at a shuffling run. Amparo caught her breath. The gringo was coming from the house whose door was painted with the colours of the roads that crossed before Xibalbá.

"Go back to the stall," she said to Inés. Women began to murmur. She felt overwhelmed by pity for her friend. Raquel's life was over. It might not even be possible for the two of them to speak again. As Willard J. Franklin vaulted into the van to applause from his fellow members of the KCKC, Amparo felt sick to her stomach. The driver revved the engine and the van drove away.

"Shameless!" Doña María said, standing on the front steps. Women hissed. Amparo turned away. On the opposite corner of the square, the door of the house remained shut.

No more tourists came. The silent alleys between the stalls reminded Amparo that Eusebio had lost his job. At four o'clock she sent Inés home to prepare supper. She bent over her loom and lifted and pulled, trying to winch the anger from her chest. Her pity for Eusebio and her rage with Raquel fused. By the time she got home, Mama would have heard that Raquel had been alone in her house with a gringo. As Raquel's friend, Amparo would be held responsible for this outrage.

The market emptied; her loneliness hardened. The sun grew lower in the sky. She carried the loom back to the stall, lowered the weavings and folded them in boxes. She closed up the stall and left the market. As she crossed the square, she avoided looking at Raquel's door.

She held her breath as she closed the door of the compound behind her and approached the house. Inside, Eusebio was curled on the sofa with his arm around Pablito. He was teaching his son to use the remote control. As if that was the lesson Pablito most needed to learn! Her husband was twice responsible for her son's timidity: he had frightened the boy in the womb and now he was passing on his passivity. He'll never get another job, she thought, watching the back of his head as he pressed the buttons. He'll never work in Antigua again. She stopped on the tiles and drew a long breath, accepting that the rest of her life would be shaped by this fact.

SIXTEEN

"*S*AKAR, RICARDO."

"*Sakar, Amparo. La utz a'wech?*"

"*Utz matiox.*" Unable to contain her curiosity, she whispered: "How was your meeting with Comandante Vladimir?"

"He agreed to teach our students." He paused, then began to read out his homework sentences. "*Ri nutata' nutik taq ixim.* My father sows corn . . . "

When he had finished, she said: "You must practise the difficult words. *B'alam.*"

"Baaalam."

"Ricardo," she said in Spanish, lowering her voice, "I wish I could see the bag you bought in Chiapas. It's such a shame you gave it to your wife."

"Not to my wife. To a friend."

His curtness took her aback. Recovering, she said: "I'm weaving a new bag. It's on the loom in the market. Would you like to visit? Later this week . . . ?"

He nodded. They returned to the lesson. The rhythm of her repetitions quelled the tension that had been prickling beneath her skin. "*Ch'op,*" she said. "Pineapple."

"Chop," he repeated.

"No, it's *ch'op.* Remember the pause after the *b* in *b'alam.* If you can't master this, you won't be able to say 'jaguar.' Now — *ch'oy.* Mouse."

"Ch'ooy," he said, almost managing it.

On the fifth repetition he succeeded. By way of contrast, she said: "*Choj*. Straight. Now try to show the difference — *ch'oy, choj*."

"Ch'ooy. *Choj*."

As he followed her instructions, she was thinking of how Eusebio was too shy to come down to Antigua to ask for work. Señor Robinson had recruited him for the drop-in centre on the recommendation of their priest. She remembered thinking: this will make my sweet, shy boy more sure of himself. But taking orders from Señor Robinson had not given him the confidence to approach other gringos. By contrast, the tables of Escuela Tecún Umán, where she had bent her head close to those of many foreigners, had built her self-confidence. Possibly she had always been more self-confident than Eusebio, but at these little tables, which creaked when you set a textbook on them, she had learned to speak on equal terms with outgoing gringa students, Evangelical missionaries who learned Spanish to flip people upside down, successful musicians with long blond hair who were planning to buy houses around Lake Atitlán, earnest skinny development workers, restrained US government employees or, now, a Canadian manager of semesters abroad. Where Eusebio saw an impregnable white wall, she perceived different types of people who needed to be addressed in different ways.

At the break, she joined the other *maestras* in the entrance hall. Luisa Méndez fixed her with a small-eyed glare. "So . . . Amparo is an *indígena*."

The younger *maestras* grew still.

"That's the only reason you're teaching the manager. Don Teófilo wouldn't let you teach Spanish to an important client — "

139

"I've taught Spanish to many im — "

"Just because this gringo wants to learn a dialect!" She shook her head, walked past the students and disappeared onto the cobblestones.

Amparo opened her mouth, then stopped: the *maestras*, being *ladinas*, would defend Luisa's prejudices. She must absorb the insult and endure, as Mayan people had been doing for five centuries. She turned to Nancy Robelo, who was wearing a pair of tight bluejeans that showed off her trim frame. "Nancy, my gringo wants to come to the village later this week. Do you want to bring yours as well?"

Nancy's eyes gleamed. "You want me to invite him?" She was such a pretty girl. Amparo couldn't understand how she had reached the age of twenty-three without marrying. In the doorway, the Canadian soldier was talking to a younger boy and a skinny *hindú* girl with glasses. "I'll invite him." Her smile widened in a way that made Amparo uneasy. "And I'm sure he'll say yes!"

After the break, she taught Ricardo how the first-person prefix for possession, *nu*, changed to *wu* when the noun started with a vowel. "*Ri nuch'op*. My pineapple. But . . . *Ri wuixin rna'j*. My mandarin orange . . . "

At noon she walked to the market and bought a piece of hot chicken in a tortilla from a stall. She was reluctant to go home. There was no hurry because Eusebio would be there when the children returned from school.

From now on, he would always be at home.

She crossed the broad Calzada by stages and wandered through the streets, marvelling, as she always did, at how there were travel agencies on every block, little hotels, restaurants, internet cafés, all housed in freshly whitewashed stucco buildings. Only the tumbled pillars of the colonial churches lacked fresh paint. She stopped at the front desks of hotels built around colonial courtyards. When she inquired about work, they looked at her in confusion. "You, señora . . . ?"

"Not for me," she explained, reassured that her black dress slacks, ironed white blouse and correct diction had made clear that such work was not for her. "It's for my husband." But in the small hotels members of the family worked behind the desk. The large hotels liked receptionists to know a little English.

It was time to go home. Children in uniforms were streaming out of the schools and spilling off the sidewalks and onto the cobblestones. At the back of the market, the Bluebird buses were idling on the dusty, potholed earth. Women were struggling up the steps with their unsold goods. Doña Rosa from the Cakchiquel Women's Savings Club, tiny and bent, dropped her bag of potatoes. A girl reached forward to catch the old woman. A shout went up, indicating that the *ayudante* had opened the bus' back door. Amparo sprinted around to the back and came face-to-face with Esperanza and her two older children. Making a cradle of her hands, she boosted Esperanza's children inside, then scrambled up behind them. She tried to remember when climbing in the back door of a school bus had ceased to be effortless. She pushed her nephew and niece against the window. Her sister pressed against her, the four of them squeezing into a seat that had been designed for two gringo schoolchildren. When the chaos subsided and the crowded bus set off up the mountain, the titter of the young people's conversation in Spanish was undercut by the soft murmur of the women's Cakchiquel.

"Did you see Doña Rosa fall?" Amparo asked.

"Poor Doña Rosa," Esperanza said. "Remember how she didn't want the school to teach in Cakchiquel?"

Amparo gripped her sister's wrist. They had been chatting in Spanish, but now she switched to Cakchiquel. "Remember how different we thought everything would be when the war ended? We thought we could have a Cakchiquel school! And a new country! The dreams we had!"

"*Ja*," Esperanza said. In Spanish, she said: "For the first two years there was some Cakchiquel in the school. Then the books began to deteriorate and they didn't replace them. The teacher spoke Cakchiquel like you or me, not like Mama or Doña Rosa. That was when I started sending my children to school in Antigua. As long as they were teaching in Cakchiquel a couple of hours a day I told myself they should study in the village so they could see their culture in a classroom, see books written in their language . . . But the world changed, Amparo. It became completely gringo. Our children won't survive with the schooling you and I had."

"That's why I send Sandra to the *colegio* — they use computers, they teach them a little English. I'm trying to save enough money to send Pablito there as well, but with Eusebio — "

Esperanza nodded. "It's expensive. Even a cheap *colegio* costs sixty quetzales a month."

"Didn't we decide to have fewer children so that we could give them more? Then I get so angry with Sandra because she doesn't know what it's like to grow up in a family of ten children! But even when I'm angry with her, I just want to give her more." She switched to Cakchiquel. "*Re'n ninjo jun chik tijob'äl pa qachab'al.* I want a little of the schooling to be in our language. I don't want her to think she's a *ladina*. I want her to succeed as a Maya. On Mayan New Year I'm going make her go to school in *traje*."

The idea occurred to her as she uttered it.

Esperanza was staring towards the front of the bus.

"What's the matter?" Amparo asked.

Esperanza laid a restraining index finger on her shoulder. "Look — "

Amparo peeped over the heads of the people around her. A very pale gringo, with shoulders as broad as a loom, sat near the front of the bus. She caught her breath. "That's the gringo that Raquel invited to her house!" she whispered in Esperanza's ear. "He speaks perfect Cakchiquel!"

"What's he doing going to our village this late in the day? The market's closing . . . "

"Oh, my poor friend!" The windows rattled in their frames. "She's ruining herself . . . "

"Who's ruining herself, Aunty Amparo?" Esperanza's daughter asked.

"You must always remember," Amparo said, looking into her niece's frank brown eyes, "that a girl must act as God orders. If you forget that, you will ruin your life!"

"I'm sure he's got a good reason for coming here," Esperanza said.

Amparo stared at the green-painted back of the seat. She had never felt so angry with Raquel.

The *ayudante* opened the back door as the bus stopped up the street from the village square. Amparo, Esperanza and the children jumped out. Amparo felt the the bus' warm black exhaust, darker than the falling dusk, soil her forearm. Women waited for the *ayudante* to unload their bags from the roof. Young men loped away, their white running shoes luminous as nighttime massed against the walls of the valley. Esperanza pulled her children against her side. "Let's wait a moment."

They backed away from the crowd. The tall gringo stepped out. Shrugging his small day backpack into the space between

143

his shoulder blades, he set off down the street towards the village square. Esperanza gathered her children against her. The gringo reached the end of the block, stopped at the house on the corner of the square and knocked on the multi-coloured door. The door opened and he slipped inside.

Amparo felt breathless. It couldn't be true! She gripped her sister's hand. "What's going to happen to her, Esperanza?" she whispered.

"He'll take her away to his country, as Yolanda's husband did."

"But her medicine, her studies . . . She needs to be here."

"Maybe the gringos like Mayan medicine. She'll starve if she stays here. After this, nobody will call her."

"She'll be driven out. Oh, my friend. *Mi pobre amiga de toda la vida . . .* "

Esperanza walked in silence. She never complained about her husband, a dull man who loaded trucks in the Antigua market and got drunk every Sunday. Reading a reproach in her sister's stolid stride, Amparo bowed her head.

Her mind staggered to grasp what was happening in the house on the corner.

It was almost dark when they unlocked the metal gate of the compound. She said a quick goodbye to her sister and her nieces. In the house, Eusebio and Pablito sat on the couch playing with the remote, switching between the news and a comedy show. Inés was late making supper. A plate on the counter contained white and dark slices of nude chicken meat nestled side by side. Amparo felt choked with anger. "Why isn't supper ready?"

"I didn't think there was any hurry."

"Well, there is a hurry. Life is hard and we all have to work. If you can't work here, you can work elsewhere. You can't just be a burden. I visited two hotels in Antigua today that are looking for girls to clean rooms. Tomorrow you and I will go to Antigua and get you a job. Sandra can do the cooking. It's time she learned to cook properly."

Sandra, who was stirring the *frijoles* on the stove, met Amparo's eyes with a hurt look.

Inés was crying. "No, señora. I've always worked — "

"You don't work enough."

She brushed past the girl to drop her bag in the bedroom. Eusebio got to his feet. "Amparo . . . "

She set down her Cakchiquel-Spanish dictionary. She was too angry to speak. If he uttered one more syllable, she would shout at him.

He regarded her with a long, half-suppressed sigh, then withdrew. Sometimes she forgot how well he knew her. The returning ebb of feeling deepened her bitterness towards Raquel. Amparo had endured trials in her marriage without losing her husband or debasing herself with other men; if Raquel was so intelligent, she should be able to do the same. Amparo sat down at the table, ignoring the stifled sobs with which Inés served the chicken, *frijoles*, avocado, and tortillas. As soon as the food was in front of them, the girl retreated to her room behind the alcove. They ate in silence. After supper, Sandra, springing to her feet, said: "Come on, Pablito, help me wash the dishes."

They put the children to bed early. Pablito fell asleep; Amparo told Sandra she could read with the light on. "Mama, will Inés have to leave?"

"Nobody's leaving. We all have to work harder."

She kissed her daughter goodnight and went to the bedroom. The room was in darkness. She could sense her husband's bulk in the bed. As she undressed she thought of flesh so white it

145

would remain visible in the deepest night. A corkscrew of heat started in her stomach and twirled up into her face and down into her thighs. She rolled into bed and clasped her husband's body against hers. She kissed him on the mouth and slid her hand down the front of his naked body.

"Amparo," he sighed with his shy laugh, "I thought you were angry with me."

After they had made love, his lovemaking meeting her expectations with the exactitude of a man who had been a husband for many years, he cradled her head in the crook of his shoulder. "Amparo, I can't spend my life in front of the television. A man has to be more than that."

"You won't find a job if you don't leave the house, Eusebio."

"What can I find? A *maquila* in the capital? I'll have to travel all night to get to work. You'll never see me. I might as well not be here."

She twisted free of his embrace and stared at him, wishing she could see the expression on his face.

"Amparo, I want to go north. I've found a *coyote*. I could stay with your brother in Phoenix . . . "

She hugged him. "¡Mi amor! It's too dangerous. They pack you into the back of a truck and you suffocate. That's what Papa says. He knows the drivers . . . "

"It doesn't have to be like that. Do you think a *mara* gang boss is packed into a truck? You can travel safely. You just have to pay for a different class of travel."

"How much do they want?"

"Forty thousand quetzales."

"Forty thousand quetzales! Eusebio, we can't — "

"I can pay it back. It's only five thousand dollars. Amparo, in the United States, any job you do, they pay you two thousand dollars a month. Two thousand dollars in a month! Here I couldn't make that in a year. Amparo, you know how many men from this village support their families by sending back money."

"And when will I see you again? Once you leave you can't come back unless you're trapped by the *migra* and come back in handcuffs, and in that case we'll have the *maras* at the door threatening our children unless we pay your debt."

"Amparo, Amparo. It's not going to be like that." When he hugged her with his whole soft body she could almost convince herself that he knew exactly how it was going to work out. "Our responsibility is to our children. If Pablito stays in that school he'll be lucky to finish the six years of primary school. We have to send him to a *colegio* in Antigua. We can't afford it unless I work."

"Inés is going out to work tomorrow."

"And how much will she bring home once she's paid her bus fare to Antigua and eaten lunch? It's not enough, Amparo."

"You're my husband, Eusebio. A husband and a wife should live together."

"Our children come before our own happiness. The *coyote's* coming to talk to me tomorrow night . . . "

The sob ambushed her. She felt her chest collapsing as though a support-post had snapped. She gasped against the shock as she realized that she had moaned aloud. Eusebio tightened his arms around her. The children, he whispered. The children . . . She had been thinking about her children since before they were born. She had rarely thought about marriage other than as the time when she would have children. Even when she had been counting down the days to her wedding night, her imagination had refused to linger on the possible delights of lovemaking, carrying her forward to the pain she would feel when her first child was born. Only now did her denial surge up to shake her like volumes of icy water, a foretaste of death that sloshed her mind around like a piece of fabric escaping from the grasp of a woman washing clothes in a river. She had disdained the happiest time of her life and now it was ending. Promising to confess her sin next Sunday, she dwelt on the pleasures she and her husband had explored in their bed. The pleasures felt insufficiently enjoyed. Though she knew she should seek a union of the spirit, her mind hummed with thoughts of two bodies wrapped together.

"Can't you find work in Antigua?"

He caressed her shoulder. She drifted into sleep.

Next morning she got on the bus with the servant girl. Doña María was sitting in front of three teenage boys in baseball caps. Her bag of potatoes tilted into the aisle. The *ayudante* hung out the door of the bus, calling, "Antigua! Antigua!" The driver went down the fitted-stone street towards the main square. As they passed the house on the corner, Doña María said: "Shameless!"

The boys in the back giggled. "The whore's shameless . . . "

"So she is," Doña María said.

Her poor friend. Amparo looked straight ahead.

"Shameless whore!" Doña María repeated with additional venom.

"She's a better *curandera* than your sister Eduviges," one boy muttered.

"She's a lot prettier," another boy said.

"Your sister's too ugly to cast spells on gringos!"

Amparo stared at her hands. How could the boys laugh off what Raquel had done? She gripped Inés' wrist. Her bad mood clung to her all the way down the mountain. In the market, she reminded the servant girl of the names of the hotels where she was told they were looking for women to clean rooms. "Come to the school at noon. I expect you to have a job."

As soon as she and Ricardo had exchanged greetings, she warned him that she couldn't invite him to the village this week. He nodded. Behind his nod she saw an emotion she could not recognize: not impatience, but an acceptance of the change in plan that felt at the same time like a form of depreciation, as though he expected her to be unreliable. She made him repeat *b'alam* until he was tripping over his tongue. In Arizona Eusebio would have to learn to talk to gringos, to stand up to them; her fear for him increased.

"*B'ey*," she said. "Road. You have to pronounce it correctly, Ricardo. *B'ey*."

"Bay," he said. "Bej. Be-ej . . . "

During the break she told Nancy Robelo that the visit to the village had been postponed. Nancy cast a sighing look in the direction of her soldier, who was talking again to the skinny *hindú* girl. Then the skinny girl veered away, and the soldier was left alone. Nancy's face lighted up.

"Don't fall in love with him, Nancy," Amparo whispered.

"I haven't. Well . . . only a little bit. It's not dangerous."

"Not for him. For you it's very dangerous."

Nancy tossed her highlighted hair. Amparo felt a heaviness wrapping around her like a damp woven blanket. It was her role today to disappoint, frustrate, and hurt; but she couldn't back down.

When she left Escuela Tecún Umán at noon, the servant girl was standing between two parked cars on the opposite side of the street. She looked away as Amparo approached. "I couldn't — "

"You couldn't what?"

"I couldn't go to the hotels. I felt ashamed."

"You didn't ask? You didn't even try to get a job? *Anchi jat jech'ël?*" she said, not caring that the girl didn't speak Cakchiquel. Across the street, the students were bantering in English as they filtered out of the school; at her feet, the boy who looked after parked cars hiccuped. "You've been hanging around the streets for four hours? You think that's more respectable than looking for a job?"

The girl bowed her head.

Amparo caught her by the shoulder of her blouse. She marched the girl past the tumbled pillars of the ruined church. At the end of the block, she let her hand drop. She felt a twinge in her heart as they passed the austere façade of Escuela San Fernando. If only Sister Consuelo had not returned to Analusia! She must rely on her own resources, and must teach this girl to do the same.

"Hurry up!" she said. The sign of Hostal Imperio Maya, the first hotel she had visited, protruded into the street. She led the girl inside. "Señora, with permission — you said you needed girls to clean the rooms. I'd like to recommend this girl to you. She has been working in my house for many years, cooking and washing and changing sheets. She is reliable and doesn't steal. We can't afford a servant any more and this girl needs work. Please, señora — "

The woman asked the girl her name, where she lived, and how long she had been working for Amparo. To Amparo's relief, the girl straightened up and answered the questions in a respectful tone. "You start at six o'clock tomorrow morning," the woman said.

"What is her wage?" Amparo asked.

The woman looked impatient. "The usual," she said and gave a figure. Amparo could hardly suppress her dismay. Inés's pay would barely cover her return bus fare to Antigua.

Where would she find the money to pay forty thousand quetzales?

She accompanied the girl as far as the Calzada. "Go home," she said, "then go to the market and open the stall. Tell Eusebio I'll be back later in the afternoon."

She walked towards the edge of town. As the cobblestones turned to tarmac, smoke from fires in the bush stung her eyes; passing trucks soiled her hair with exhaust. She hadn't phoned Yolanda, taking for granted that she would be at home. Her mind turned to Doña Manuela's divination. If Doña Manuela was correct, finding a way for Eusebio to work in the north might be the most important job of her life.

The guard slouching in the new security hut at the edge of the development waved her past. As she knocked on the door of her sister's house, the Santa María dialect with which Doña Manuela spoke Cakchiquel ran through her mind. Her brother-in-law answered. "Yes?"

She caught her breath, intimidated by his height, by the flat stomach and vigorous shoulders that looked as though they had been transplanted from the body of a younger man. His spray of greying curls belied the crooked, handsome severity of his face. "I'm Amparo. Yolanda's oldest sister."

"Of course. Yolanda . . . your sister . . . "

"Amparo!" She heard the sound of Yoli's feet on the tiles. The hug she longed for enfolded her in Yoli's youth and warmth and energy. And gratitude, Amparo felt: she was still the only member of the family who visited Yoli.

They led her into the living room and sat her on the couch. David turned off the television and pointed towards the window. "You see that security hut? I told them to build it. I told them their security is *mierda*. I'm going to keep telling them until they make this development into a place where I can leave my wife in safety."

Amparo nodded. She took a covert glance at the candlestick on the shelf, its curves deflecting the afternoon sunlight. A Mayan woman she didn't recognize brought in a can of Coca-Cola and a glass on a tray. "Where's Doña Manuela?" Amparo asked.

"Who?" David said, stretching his long legs.

Yoli looked stricken. "We had to let her go."

"The servant?" David said. "She was a disaster. I came home and there were seeds on the floor and my menorah had been desecrated. She performed some kind of savage ritual in my living room," he said, waving his arm to encompass the space he owned.

Yolanda left the room.

"So, Amparo," David said, settling into an armchair. He had wiry wrinkles in the corners of his mouth. "What can we do for you? How are things going in the family?"

She had to tell him, even if it meant being demolished by his scorn. She felt her hand tremble as she drank from the glass of Coca-Cola.

"My mother is well, my father still enjoys driving trucks . . . " She saw his impatience as he picked at the whorls of black hair that covered the backs of his hands up to the knuckles. Forcing herself to think of her children, she said: "Eusebio has lost his job."

Yoli returned to the room and sat down next to her husband. Hurrying on, afraid that they would blame Eusebio, Amparo explained that the funding for Señor Robinson's NGO had been cut, that the Americans were sending all their money to the Arabs now.

"You have to understand, Amparo," David said, his hands parting. "This war the Americans are going to fight in Iraq is a war that must be fought. No one knows that better than people of my race."

She hurried on, speaking of the importance of her children's education, of the impossibility of her husband's finding another job in Antigua or Guatemala City. Finally she told them of Eusebio's decision, of how much the *coyote* was going to cost. "We don't have the money. That's why," she said, hearing her voice going hoarse, "I've come to ask — "

"Amparo! We can't give you forty thousand quetzales!" Yoli was on her feet. "How's David supposed to feel if my relatives ask him for money? Do you want him to think we're all beggars?"

Amparo stared at the coffee table. Not even Yoli had escaped their mother's legacy of shame.

"A *coyote* doesn't have to cost forty thousand quetzales. You can get one cheaper than that."

"Eusebio doesn't want to risk his life."

"You don't have to pay the money up front. Everyone knows the *maras* will give you a loan."

"A loan from the *maras* is too dangerous. If Eusebio is sent back, they'll make my daughter into a prostitute to pay off the loan."

"Amparo!" Yoli reached for Amparo's glass of Coca-Cola, picked it up and drained it. "I thought I'd got away from these problems!" She sat down in the chair, her hair falling over her face. "I'm sorry, David. I apologize for my family!" She and David started to make incomprehensible sounds. The sight of her little sister, who had been so neglectful of her studies, holding a conversation in English made Amparo feel small and backward. Every time she tried to improve her life, shame lay in wait for her like a malevolent spirit.

David leaned forward, clasping his hands between his knees. "I've been telling my wife that we're responsible for our family. That doesn't mean we hand out money to every relative who asks, but in the case of you and your husband, who have a plan to improve your situation . . . " He shrugged his shoulders. "If you're going to have a debt, it's better that it be with us than with the *maras*." He concentrated on her face. "Where does your husband want to go?"

"Phoenix, Arizona. Our brother — "

"Yes, of course, your brother. I could arrange for your husband to travel to Phoenix. But it's better if I don't get involved. I have to rely on this terrible government of Portillo for business. Find yourself a reliable *coyote*. Yoli and I will pay. But, you listen to me," he said, gesturing with his right hand as his face shook into a jagged smile, "as soon as your husband gets to Phoenix, he pays us back. I expect regular payments!"

"¡Sí, *Don David! No se preocupe*. You'll be proud of us, I promise!" She leaned forward to kiss his hand, her knee grazing the floor. His dark whorls tickled her lips. "Thank you so much! God will bless you!"

"Get me a blessing from a Mayan god," he said, with a laugh.

David drank a rum and Coke to celebrate the loan. Amparo tried in vain to meet her sister's eyes. Yoli wouldn't speak to her. She had woven David, Yoli's banner of escape, into the family tapestry. Wary of an argument that might jeopardize the loan, she thanked David and Yoli, and promised to call them once Eusebio had confirmed his arrangements with the *coyote*. As she walked along the edge of the tarmac road back to Antigua, smoke stung her eyes.

Her misery clung to her all through supper. She and Eusebio had arranged to send the children to see her parents before the *coyote* could arrive. After supper, Sandra led Pablito out the door by the hand. Amparo ordered Inés to go to her room. "You have to get up early tomorrow."

The girl hesitated, then retreated in silence.

She and Eusebio pulled back chairs from the table. She looked at him, unable to imagine the house without him. Finally she said: "I went to see Yoli and David today. David said he would lend us the money."

"You're joking, Amparo! You did that? He said yes?"

"He said yes." She was relieved that his reaction was as stifled as hers. Any sign of delight would wound her. Yet beneath his self-control, she detected a sheen of fear. She suspected that, like her, he had been secretly hoping that they would not find the money.

He went to the phone and called the *coyote*. "He says he'll come by at nine o'clock to discuss arrangements," he said, as he hung up.

They sat at the table, looking at each other, examining each other's faces and saying little, until Eusebio said: "It's nine o'clock."

They went outside. The pale wash of light from her family's houses around the compound darkened the dust of the courtyard. She listened to the silence.

A knock on the gate. Amparo opened it. A small man entered, hunched in spite of his youth. She did not know what she had expected a *coyote* to look like but this man appeared too ordinary to conjure people across borders. She led him towards the house. He followed. His right foot hung behind his left with a limping, heel-dragging step. She watched the side of his shoe rasp the dirt. She felt sick to her stomach. Afraid she might faint, she sat down on a low stucco wall. Eusebio and the *coyote* looked at her. "Go ahead," she whispered. "Go inside. I'll be there in a minute."

The *coyote* looked at Eusebio. "What's wrong with her?"
Eusebio shrugged his shoulders. "Women . . . "
She watched the two men walk towards the house.

SEVENTEEN

EVERY NIGHT SHE EDGED HER leg across the mattress to the space that belonged to his knee. She fanned her calf over the sheet, summoning his presence as she did the presence of God or Ixmucane. But Eusebio was a man, and once a man was gone he could not be recalled. Having conceived of her marriage as a bond bestowed by God, a pact the two of them had made with their Church, she remembered their years together as his snores, the smell of his chest, the weight of his hand on her stomach and her thighs, his shy nibbling of her nipples, the sweat that plastered them together. His voice on the phone, during the ten minutes' conversation they allowed themselves every Sunday night, belonged to another man, a husband in name and obligation but not in body. Their marriage had turned into a balloon that floated high above her, while her daily life went its own way down on earth.

The night he left, the *coyote* had come at 3:00 AM. She had put Sandra and Pablito to bed, then returned to the couch, where he was watching a *telenovela* at low volume. She took the remote control from his hand. "Are you going to say goodbye to Sandra and Pablito?"

He shook his head with the little-boy shyness that never failed to strike a pang into her heart. "I can't say goodbye to my children, Amparo."

She let these words hang in the air for a very long time. She put the remote control on the coffee table and took his hand in hers. "It's better this way," he said.

His tranquillity frightened her, as though he were already in another country. Once a man went north, he stayed there unless he returned in handcuffs. The good men continued to send money to the Western Union office in Antigua, but many had other wives, other families, up there. At least that would not happen to them. Eusebio would be staying with her brother. He was leaving the country, but not the family. Nor was he going away forever; of that she felt certain. Yet his calm provoked her until, acting as she had rarely acted in all the years they had been married, she said: "If you're not saying goodbye to the children, you can come and say goodbye to me."

In the bedroom, she left a lamp on, wanting him to see the light glimmering on her breasts as they made love, wanting him to remember her with all his senses to cancel out the possibility of another woman making an impression there. She felt brazen and shameless. Later, when the digital clock flipped to 1:00 AM as her husband dozed on his back, she took him in her mouth as a *señora decente* did not do, and teased out his pleasure with an avidness that no number of Hail Marys would exonerate until he woke with a moan, raging to make love with her one more time.

At 3:00 AM, she held his hand as they walked to the gate of the compound. Her husband gave her a kiss and left. She locked the gate, walked back into the house, went to her bedroom and turned out the light. Each morning now, she woke to the stunned awareness of his absence. The pain clung to her, as persistent as the ache in Mama's back.

For two days she heard nothing. On the third night, after the children were in bed, her brother Rafael called from Phoenix. "Sister, I have someone here who wants to talk to you."

"*Llegué al lugar indicado*," Eusebio said. A chill passed through her at the sound of this phrase. More than the tinny murmur of Rafael's gringoized Spanish, the phrase *llegar al lugar indicado*, to arrive at the appropriate place — because the *coyotes* forbade their clients from uttering the names of their destinations — told her that her husband was in the USA. As though it were the most natural thing in the world for Eusebio to travel, she asked him about his trip. "Really smooth," he said. He had driven north with the *coyote* and two other men. By morning they had reached Huehuetenango. Somewhere north of this northwestern city the four-by-four had turned onto a pitted sideroad, then another. Eusebio and another man were told to get out and walk over the hill in front of them. Two hours later, as they stumbled through the rocks and dust of this land too arid for agriculture, and came down the far side of the incline, they saw the four-by-four waiting for them in a ravine. "Welcome to Mexico," the *coyote* said when they got to the door. He handed them Mexican ID cards that bore their photographs. They drove to Tuxtla Gutiérrez, the capital of Chiapas, and booked into a hotel. "The rooms had showers," Eusebio said. "In the morning we went downstairs and there were gringos eating breakfast in the dining room!" After breakfast, Eusebio and the other man were driven to the airport —

"You took a plane?"

"Two!" They had flown from Tuxtla to Mexico City, then from Mexico City to Monterrey. She peppered him with questions. What had it felt like to fly? "No, Amparo, there isn't time," he said, leaving her with a chastened resentment of the authority conferred on him by his new knowledge. In

Monterrey they took away his Mexican ID card and gave him an American passport with his photograph and another man's name. He was put in the back seat of a car full of Mexican-Americans from San Antonio, Texas returning from a shopping trip in Mexico. They spent the night in a motel on the outskirts of San Antonio. In the morning they took away his passport and gave him a bus ticket to Phoenix. Rafael and Megan picked him up at the station.

"When do you start working? Eusebio, I need money to send Pablito to school in Antigua!"

"Give me a moment, Amparo!"

In the morning, after Inés had left, Sandra and Pablito played with their food. "Where's Papa?" Sandra asked.

"He's with Uncle Rafael and Aunt Megan," Amparo said. She watched the children considering this information.

"Is he happy there?" Sandra said.

"He's happy because he will be able to work and send us money."

They nodded their heads in understanding. Other children's fathers were doing this. They did not ask about him again.

She worked in the market in the afternoons, weaving in front of her stall. She finished the red bag with the sauntering white jaguar on the front. She wasn't happy with it: the crook of the jaguar's foreleg was wrong. To convey a sense of perspective, she had woven a white mountain into the background near the top of the bag. Examining the finished product, she saw that the mountain was too far away from the jaguar: rather than investing him with a sense of movement, the hump made him look as though he had strayed far from home. She stored the bag in the back of the stall, reluctant to display it.

The Canadian students' month of intensive language courses had ended, and with them her morning sessions with Ricardo. Don Teófilo's next contract was with the State Department of the United States. Amparo was one of the *maestras* he retained for this assignment. She had taught State Department officials before: they were humourless, competent men who learned Spanish vocabulary efficiently but seemed to feel that it was impertinent of her to suggest that they alter their Yanqui accents when speaking Spanish. This time she had been assigned to teach a man from a special unit of the US Marines. Ricardo had paid Don Teófilo to continue his Cakchiquel classes twice a week; he had agreed to schedule the classes in the afternoon now that her mornings were full. She had just enough time for a quick lunch of tortilla and avocado between the two students. She returned to her desk in the front room of Escuela Tecún Umán as he came in the door.

"*Sakar, Ricardo.*"

"*Sakar, Amparo. La utz a'wech?*"

In Spanish he asked her about her new morning student. As she heard herself venting her disgust, she realized how much she had come to trust Ricardo. "He boasts he can go into the jungle . . . into the jungle *naked*." She faltered. "He says he can feed and clothe himself from roots and branches. He knows how to kill men with his bare hands. Oh, he's ugly . . . Tattoos everywhere, and he has three girlfriends in Guatemala City. He expects me to listen to such filth! He can speak quite a lot of Spanish, but such language! Usually the gringos from the State Department are very correct, but this man's a *kaibil*."

She trusted that he had spent enough time in Guatemala to know that *kaibiles* were special forces units that had committed massacres during the civil war. He nodded. "How long are you going to be teaching him?"

"Until his next assignment starts." She leaned forward. "Ricardo, when he leaves I may not be able to continue teaching you. I don't mind coming to Antigua if I have four hours with the *kaibil*. Then the extra two hours make sense. But to come to Antigua just for two hours' work . . . " Eager to avoid any hint of a rebuff, she said: "You must come and visit our market. I'm sorry I had to cancel before, but there were problems in my family."

"I'd be delighted to visit your market," he said.

On the afternoons when she wasn't teaching Ricardo, she returned from her morning classes with the *kaibil* disheartened. The empty house desolated her. With the children at school and Inés in Antigua, she felt abandoned. She would turn on the television and imagine that Eusebio was sitting beside her on the couch, fantasies that led to feverish imaginings which she stifled in sobs. She had never thought of herself as weak, but now she feared that she had grown too used to being married. Her longing for Eusebio backed up into resentment of him for having spoiled her with his constant weight in bed. She went out into the yard of the compound, where Papa, if he wasn't away on a delivery, would sit smoking a cigarette. Mama winnowed black beans in a woven basket. She sat with them. In their solemn way Mama and Papa allotted her more time than before, encouraging her in the gentlest of tones to go to the market, where she might make a sale. The sight of them sitting side by side, made her dizzy at the thought of the thousands of kilometres of mountain and desert separating her from Eusebio. Her marriage had filled with unstaunchable space. More and more, her thoughts concentrated on how to bring her family together again.

Mayan New Year approached. Mama burned incense on the day, but ignored the customs she had learned in childhood for fear of angering the priest. Amparo felt restless. She conserved her marriage in every atom of her daily life, yet, to her guilty dismay, the fading of Eusebio's presence gave her moments of elated freedom. She could be as Maya as she wished without offending her *ladino* husband. She could raise the children according to her will alone.

"Sandra," she said, "on Mayan New Year, you will wear *traje* to school."

"Regular *traje*? Or is there a special *traje* for the New Year?"

Exasperated, Amparo blurted: "I don't know . . . I'll find out."

Sandra stood up, twisting her thickening hips in the elastic little-girl slacks that were too small for her. "How are you going to find out?"

"I'll ask someone," Amparo said. She laid her hand on Pablito's shoulder. The boy sat at the table drawing a picture. Figures in long gowns stood on a steep-pitched mountain landscape. The burning orb overhead looked like the sun, but when she asked him, trying to divert Sandra's questions, he said it was the moon. "*Ri ik'*," he said shyly, startling her by remembering the Cakchiquel word for moon. The longing in his nervous eyes made her shiver.

"Yes, the moon," she said, in Spanish.

Sandra sidled up to her, looping her arm around Amparo's hip and gazing at Pablito's drawing. "I bet," she said, "that you'll have to ask Raquel. Raquel knows more about *traje* than you do . . . " Amparo ignored her. Pablito reached for his red crayon. Sandra continued: "Did you and Raquel have a fight, Mama? Aren't you best friends any more . . . ?"

"Of course we're best friends! It's not like you and the girls at school, changing your minds every week about who you're friends with. Women support each other, indigenous women in the same community . . . "

"Then why don't you ask her?"

163

"All right, we'll go see Raquel right now! Pablito, come on, we're — "

"I want to finish my drawing!" Pablito wailed.

She took Pablito to Esperanza's house and left him to draw. She tried to persuade Sandra, too, to stay with Esperanza. "No," Sandra said with a dark stare. "I want to hear what Raquel says."

Amparo spied Esperanza biting down on a smile. She hustled Sandra out the door. They closed the gate of the compound behind them and walked to the house on the corner of the square.

The brightly coloured door opened and Raquel looked out with a vexed expression. They had barely spoken since Pablito's illness. As she stepped inside, Amparo was aware of Sandra watching her with furious scrutiny. She felt a nervous twist as the narrow walls enclosed her in the first smudge of evening. Below the poster of the Mayan ceremonial calendar, a postcard glowed in the day's last light. Amparo saw a photograph of a skyscraper-studded skyline and the words *Kansas City*.

Raquel gave her a look of disregard that sheered into glancing defiance. Amparo became so angry that, until her daughter nudged her hip, she forgot why they had come. "My daughter," she said in Cakchiquel, "wants to dress in *traje* for New Year's day — "

"*You* want me to wear *traje*," Sandra said in Spanish.

" — and we do not know if she needs a special *traje*, or if ordinary *traje* is enough."

She stopped, conscious of the shuddering in her voice. Raquel stared at her. "Your *traje* tells the history of your village. Do you need more than that?"

"I don't know what I need," Amparo said in exasperation. "I came here because I thought you were my friend."

164

"Are you still my friend, Amparo? Now that you're alone, do you understand that women have to act on their fantasies?"

"I understand where my duty lies." She tightened her grip on Sandra's wrist.

Raquel smiled. "You will always be a Catholic."

Amparo was aware that she had not invited them to sit down. Raquel seemed impatient; although alone, she felt occupied. "How is your son?" she asked.

"He's better. Thank you."

"If he wants to train as a Mayan priest, I'm willing to help him."

"Oh, Pablito just wants to be a *käk winaq* like his father. I'll be happy if my daughter learns our traditions to pass them on to her daughter." Fearing that she had sounded offhand, she looked down at Sandra, who stared back at her with an expression that was too contradictory to fathom. Amparo let herself out of the house.

In the cool silence of the empty square in front of the closed-up market, they felt alone. Sandra said: "Mama, Raquel looks like a witch."

"She's a *curandera*, a medicine woman."

"No, Mama, a witch! Like those three sisters on television who are witches."

Amparo, remembering the program Sandra was referring to, balked. Could her daughter understand what a *curandera* did only by comparing Raquel to a gringo TV series? Her children's world was too complicated. It would clear Sandra's mind to wear *traje* to school.

As she opened the gate of the compound, she prepared to tell Eusebio about the visit and realized for the five hundredth time that he had disappeared. The man who spoke to her on the telephone for ten minutes on Sunday night, with his know-it-all

165

brusqueness and evasions, was not the gentle Eusebio to whom she used to spill out the events of her day.

On Mayan New Year, she woke up early, helped Sandra with her bath, braided her hair, then dressed her. She had let out the waist of Sandra's black skirt and bought her a new *huipil* in the market. She slid the woven headband over the braids, then led her beautiful girl, groomed and glimmering, out into the compound to see her grandmother. Mama fell mute. Amparo felt mortified at her mother's silence: if Mama wasn't feeling shame for being an Indian, she was feeling shame for not being Indian enough.

The minibus that went to the *colegios* in Antigua honked outside the compound. Amparo waved goodbye to Sandra, then prepared for her class with the gringo *kaibil*.

In the afternoon, when Sandra came home, she said: "Señora Machojón is ignorant!" Señora Machojón was her teacher. "In class this morning, Señora Machojón said, 'Oh, Sandra. Don't tell me you're a little *indianita*! I thought you were a civilized girl!'"

Amparo caught her breath. "What did you say?"

"*Me puse tan brava, Mama* . . . I got so furious . . . I said, 'My Mama says that we were here first and we had a great civilization and your Spanish conquistadors didn't even know how to read and write, and this isn't your country!'"

Amparo's face felt hot. She hugged her daughter and felt as though Sandra were comforting her. "Two other girls in my class wore *traje* today. The other girls didn't talk to us after what I said. They're not my friends anymore."

"Keep your *traje* on," she said. "We'll get Pablito and go to the market and open the stall for an hour before supper." She felt the need to surround Sandra with a circle of Mayan women.

166

That week a Honduran soccer team played at El Pensativo football stadium. They visited the village before the game. Amparo sold three simple woven bags and a waistcoat streaming with artificial colours. She made no more sales that week. Every day there were fewer tourists; the gringos were staying at home as their country geared up for war. The market was silent for hours. On Thursday night Yolanda phoned to ask about Eusebio. Amparo, hearing in her question a demand to know when the forty thousand quetzales would be repaid, felt flustered that her little sister could make her feel guilty. During their Sunday night phone call, she had begged him to find a job.

"You don't understand how hard it is," he said. "I don't have documents, I don't speak English . . . "

Before their ten minutes had elapsed, they had hung up.

EIGHTEEN

"OUR HOMES ARE LIKE BOWLS and . . . *Chupam ri läq re' niqatij qaq'utun!*"

Seeing the young women knit their brows, Amparo repeated in Spanish: "Within this bowl we eat our food! Our husbands must work so that the bowl is full for our children."

"*Ja!*" Doña Rosa said in agreement. The last village mother of her generation, since the death of Doña Juana two years earlier, she sat on the couch. Amparo had pushed the television into the corner and laid cushions on the floor for the younger women. She herself sat in a wicker chair. Sandra and Pablito, sitting at the kitchen table, watched the women over their homework.

The Cakchiquel Women's Savings Club had almost perished after the robbery. Many of the women had stopped attending, pulled their children out of school to work in the *milpa*, and bowed their heads before their husbands' recriminations at the money they had lost. Led by Raquel, the Evangelicals had deserted. The gringo in the purple T-shirt had said that this would destroy them. Amparo could not stand the thought that he might be right. "We must start again," she told the women. She held Pablito at her breast; she was weak and exhausted. They all trembled at each creak in the back room of the church. But, supported by the señora gringa and the joy that made life vivid as she and Eusebio began to live as husband and wife again, she went from house to house persuading women that they must go on.

The señora gringa had suggested changes that would strengthen their association. No longer would their savings be withdrawn from the bank in Antigua before each meeting. A bank statement would replace cash; the women would learn to trust documents. This, the señora gringa said, would be a step in understanding civil society. Each meeting would take place in a different house. Three different women would be authorized to deposit money in the account; the responsibility of carrying the month's savings down the mountain to Antigua and returning with a validated deposit slip would rotate among these women. The señora gringa ensured that the government matching funds were maintained. After President Arzú left office, the new FDR government of young Portillo and old Ríos Montt had intensified the scrutiny of their accounting procedures. The village's FDR mayor demanded still more paperwork. In spite of the problems, they kept their matching funds. Six years later, their numbers hovered just below the membership at the time of the robbery. The presence of young women in their early twenties had changed the club. These women wished to discuss relations between husband and wife in ways that made Doña Rosa bow her head in shame, and sometimes brought a blush even to the cheeks of Amparo and Esperanza; they understood Cakchiquel but addressed the meeting in Spanish. A year after the robbery the señora gringa had left for another country, as gringos always left for other countries, and two years later Amparo had learned of Don Julio's death from throat cancer. Under her guidance the smaller, more cautious Cakchiquel Women's Savings Club had built up its assets to seven hundred American dollars, more than twice its holdings at the time of the robbery. They were beginning to make their first micro-credit grants. Amparo wished she could show the señora gringa or Don Julio or Sister Consuelo what she had achieved; but they had all vanished, and now Eusebio, her audience and counsel, was gone as well.

"We can barely feed our daughter," a girl in her early twenties said. "What will happen when I have more children?"

"Have fewer children," Amparo said, "and bring them up well — "

"We both work! If we didn't live with my parents we'd starve."

"We live with my husband's parents," another girl said. "It's terrible, six of us in two rooms. My husband and I are never alone — "

"If you're never alone, you won't have too many children!" the first girl replied.

Doña Rosa looked at her gnarled feet. Amparo doubted that she had understood their swift Spanish. She hoped that Sandra would not understand either, although this was less likely.

"My husband wants to go north," the first girl said.

"Our task is to remain here, strengthen our community and promote our culture." Amparo couldn't go on. She wasn't afraid of having her husband's absence pointed out; she no longer knew what to say.

"I'd be terrified if my husband went north," the second girl said. "Look at that poor *muchacho* — "

"What sadness for his mother," Doña Soledad said. "She thinks her son is safe in the north, then he's dead. Did you see that poor woman's face?"

For days television had been covering the life of the first American soldier killed in Iraq, a boy from Guatemala City. The boy had been told that he could stay in the United States if he signed on with the Army. Amparo saw Esperanza's discreet look of concern. But she had no fear that Eusebio . . . he wasn't a soldier.

"It's not just war," the second girl said. "They find other women. You can't be apart for that long — "

"Not my Juan — "

Not my Eusebio . . . May God spare him from the Army and other women. Esperanza glanced at her. She remained silent before the murmur of Doña Soledad summarizing the girls' exchange for Doña Rosa in Cakchiquel.

"The best way," the second girl said, "would be to bring the gringos and their money here so that our men don't have to go there."

"But it's women who earn money from tourism," Esperanza said. "We're the ones who work in the markets, the hotels, the language schools. We have the opportunity to maintain our families and our culture. Our men get paid as manual workers, whether they stay here or go north."

"We need to have more gringos give us money," Doña Soledad said. "Look at Raquel. She's going to have a baby from that gringo. He'll give her money for sure."

"Raquel has ruined herself!" Amparo said. "She's bound by her marriage vows before God. Now she'll have to leave the village and live on the street in the capital until she dies in misery. That gringo won't pay her a centavo!"

Her face was drenched with heat. The girls looked terrified; she hoped she had frightened Sandra just as badly. She glared out over the room, enforcing a silence that stilled even Doña Rosa's light breathing.

Doña Soledad, meeting Amparo's eyes, said in a soft voice: "I'd trust a gringo to support a child before I'd trust a lot of our men."

"Since we're talking about money," Amparo said, "has everyone got their six quetzales? *Qonojel q'o waqi' quetzal?*"

They counted the money. This week it was her turn to take the quetzales to the bank and return with a deposit slip. She put the money in a leather bag. Next morning, when she arrived at Escuela Tecún Umán, Don Teófilo told her that her *kaibil* had been reassigned by his government. Against her will, her mind filled with a vision of the huge white man stalking naked through the jungle, his tattoos illuminated by the light falling through the canopy. Relief outweighed her dismay at her lost income.

"Of course, you still have your course with Ricardo this afternoon."

"But, Don Teófilo, I can't come to Antigua for two hours. It's too little money. And especially not in the afternoon, when my children are coming home from school!"

Don Teófilo regarded her from behind his large, square glasses. "If you wish to cancel your course with Don Ricardo, you have my permission. But I have very little work to offer, Amparo. I had another contract cancelled yesterday because twenty gringo students decided to stay at home."

"I can't come for two hours' work. I'm better off selling my weaving in the market."

She went to the bank, deposited the money, then sat in the park. Antigua's empty streets looked sad, in spite of the glare of bright sunlight on the white stucco buildings. In the afternoon she returned to the school, sat down opposite Ricardo, and explained that, having lost her morning class, she could no longer teach him in the afternoons. His pinched face, turned a pinkish shade of brown by its exposure to the sun, grew stiff for a moment. She imagined Eusebio quailing before gringo would-be employers. "Life here is hard, Ricardo. Unless I work for four hours, I can't afford to come to Antigua."

She watched his head nod. Like all gringo men, he was used to getting his way. Tenderness filled her as she recalled Eusebio's understanding of limitations. She felt discomfort that her greatest closeness was with a man who had become a ghost. The hectoring voice on the telephone on Sunday nights belonged to someone with gringo impatience and gringo expectations but no gringo dollars. She wasn't certain that she would make more money in the market. She would simply spare herself the bus fare to Antigua and the difficulty of teaching Cakchiquel classes, which, unlike Spanish classes, required preparation. She would spend more time in her community which, in Eusebio's absence, had become more important to her. "I hope you will come to visit me, Ricardo. Maybe next week?"

For his last lesson, she taught him the verb to pay: *nintoj, natoj, nutoj* . . . "Now we'll learn how to form this verb with direct and indirect objects. *Reje' yetijoj* . . . They pay it. *Reje' yetojon* . . . They pay him or her . . . "

"They do not pay you," he said.

She paused. The curl in the corner of his mouth was unexpected, as his humour was always unexpected. His joke woke her up to the closeness that had woven them together during their hours at this table. They laughed in the coarse, carefree way she might laugh with her brothers. He was a manager, a man of influence. She wanted to show him her stall in the market, to invite him to the compound and her house. But, in order for her to do this, he could not come alone. "Bring one or two of the students when you visit. We can eat lunch at my house."

She left Antigua aware that she would be spending less time there over the coming weeks. For the next few mornings she went to the village market and wove on the concrete floor in front of her stall. In the absence of tourists, the women turned to gossip. The mayor was going to raise licence fees for stalls; it was said he was going to deny licences to women who did not support the FDR party. Doña María's daughter's husband had gone north; Raquel's pregnancy was starting to show, she had bought new furniture, imagine the dollars her gringo must be sending her!

She waited for the condemnation of Raquel to reach a pitch. Yet, contrary to all that life in this village had taught her, no one seemed outraged by Raquel's crime.

On Saturday Ricardo phoned. "I can't visit you. We have a problem in our program . . . But thank you very much for the invitation. I'll call you as soon as I have more time . . . *Xaj*," he said, adding the Cakchiquel salutation to the Spanish excuses which had flowed as if he had practised them.

"*Xaj*," she said, feeling a tug of sadness. Would he remember her, as Don Julio had remembered her, if a year from now she needed his help? She felt a shift inside her, emotion altering its expectations as she began to look forward to her Sunday night phone call from Eusebio.

On Sunday, as his voice filled her ear, something had changed. "I got a job, Amparo!" He would be putting groceries in bags at a supermarket check-out. She asked how soon he would be able to send money. "I have to pay the money I owe your brother. Give me time to get on my feet!"

"All right." She felt her fierceness relent. During the rest of the conversation, each time she mentioned the children, she heard him receiving her words as a reproof. The next week a van containing German tourists arrived and she sold the jaguar bag with the awkward foreleg. She wove wall-hangings of quetzal birds with the word "*Guatemala*" running along the top because she could make them quickly and sell them quickly. She avoided starting another bag. One day she realized that more than a month had passed since she had stopped teaching at Escuela Tecún Umán. White clouds built up in the afternoon sky. The sharp-edged light had blurred. In a month the rains would come. That Sunday Eusebio told her that soon he would send her money to put Pablito in a *colegio* in Antigua. "And the debt?" she said. "My sister wants to know when we're going to pay back the forty thousand quetzales."

He fell silent, then brought the call to a close.

Two days later, Ricardo phoned and apologized for not having been in touch. "Would it be all right if I came to see your market this week?"

"Is your wife visiting you?"

"No." In a soft voice, he said: "She may not come to visit me here."

Thinking fast, she said: "You're welcome to visit, Ricardo. I'll invite Nancy Robelo, you remember? I know she'd like to invite her student, the soldier . . . "

"Brett," Ricardo said.

"Yes, the three of you can take the bus together." She had run into Nancy near Escuela Tecún Umán one day when she had gone to Antigua. Nancy was pining for her soldier. Knowing that the Canadians were still in Antigua made her loneliness worse. She had seen the soldier once in the park, she admitted. When she tried to call out to him, her voice had crumpled in her throat. Amparo felt touched by this beautiful girl's confession of weakness. "I'll talk to Nancy and call you back."

When she phoned the next day, he sounded guarded. "Thursday at one in the afternoon," he repeated, after she'd told him that Nancy would meet him in front of Escuela Tecún Umán.

"You must invite the soldier."

"Brett," he said again, with a coolness that unsettled her.

The plan felt uncertain. She was surprised when, a little before two o'clock on Thursday, Ricardo, Nancy, and Brett got down from the bus on the edge of the village square and walked towards the market.

"*Sakar*, Amparo," Ricardo said. "*La utz a'wech?*"

"*Utz matiox. Y ret?*" His affable tone cancelled out the curtness of their phone conversations, reminding her of the confidences they had shared. His face, at once round and narrow, had turned redder with more prolonged exposure to the sun; his brown hair glistened with a sun-stroked shade of blond that contained flickers of grey. As Nancy and Brett swept past them in a burst of giggles, he replied in Cakchiquel that he was well, then asked her in Spanish to show him the market. She led him towards her stall at the back. Offended by Nancy's loud laughter — as her guest, Nancy's behaviour would reflect on her — she whispered: "*Maestras* must be very careful not to fall in love with their students. But she admitted to me that she fell in love with him."

He stared at her, the blueness of his eyes harder than usual. "I hope it doesn't become a problem. We have enough problems already."

"Nancy's a very respectable girl," she said, taken aback.

Nancy's laughter echoed from the next aisle. Amparo heard the rush of her feet. Breathless, her eyes brilliant, she came around the corner. The soldier followed her. Beneath the force of Ricardo's stare, the young man dropped his hand from Nancy's elbow. The couple came to a halt, breathing too hard. Ricardo asked the soldier in Spanish if he'd bought any

176

handicrafts: "You should buy something while you're here." He continued in English. The soldier nodded.

Nancy, sliding out of the tall young man's reach, said: "Are we going to your house to meet your husband, Amparo?"

"My husband's away at work," Amparo said in a murmur, hoping the women at the nearby stalls wouldn't overhear her. "He'd been unemployed for a long time, so he got a job in a *maquila*. He starts work at seven in the morning and doesn't come back until late at night."

Ricardo looked taken aback. Nancy was observing her with a sly expression. "What a shame," she said. "Come on, Brett. Let's look at the handicrafts. Are you going to buy me something?"

Amparo watched her go, surprised to find that she no longer liked Nancy. The soldier's attention had turned her head.

"Show me your weaving," Ricardo said. "I want to see the jaguar. Then I'll know whether the bag I bought in Chiapas was made by you."

"Oh, Ricardo, I sold it! Some tourists — "

"You don't have any more?"

"I'll weave more. I'll show them to you next year."

"I hope I'll be here."

A stroke of fear crossed her chest. "You work here, no?"

He looked at the concrete floor. "Our program's not going well."

The edge in his voice unsettled her. This would mean less work at Escuela Tecún Úmán. Having lost Sister Consuelo, Don Julio and the señora gringa, she did not want to lose Ricardo. "But you'll stay here . . . You're living in Antigua . . . "

Fingering one of the wall hangings, he said: "My wife can't visit me here. She travels a lot for work."

He shrugged his shoulders with a helpless gesture that reminded her of Eusebio's gestures at the time they had married. Her breath tightened in her throat. "Ricardo," she whispered, "I'm so sorry. What I just said was a lie. My husband doesn't work in a *maquila*. He went to the United States." At the sight of his astonishment, she said: "I felt so bad lying with you standing there. I thought, 'How can I lie to Ricardo . . . ?' But I can't tell Nancy. She might tell Don Teófilo and he knows the police and gringos from the State Department . . . "

He nodded, the blueness of his eyes shining with candour. "Did you have to pay a *coyote* . . . ?"

"Yes, we had to pay a *coyote*."

Ricardo asked her more questions in a very soft voice. He backed off two steps. "So my wife is in another country and so is your husband. *Ret jatq'o ayo'n, re'n jinq'o ayon.* You are alone and I am alone."

"*Ja*," she said, her voice a single cautious breath. Heat rose through her body; his Cakchiquel drew him hideously close to her.

"Our students' semester here is over. Brett and the others," he said, gesturing over his shoulder, as he continued in Spanish, "will be going home next week."

"Does Nancy know . . . ?"

"I assume Brett's told her . . . "

She felt a pulse of concern. "I'll make sure she knows."

"I have some free time before the next group arrives." He shook his body in a way that made her feel the length of his gringo limbs. "I'm going to take a trip across the north of the country, from Cobán to Nebaj . . . "

"I went to Nebaj with my brother and my husband. Be careful, Ricardo. There were all sorts of terrible people on the bus — *ex-guerrilleros, ex-kaibiles* . . . " Wondering why he was

178

making this trip rather than going to see his wife, she asked: "And when you come back . . . ?"

"*Re'n ninjo jinq'o pa Antigua. Re'n manäq iwatan si ri nusamaj . . .* " He wanted to be in Antigua but he didn't know if his work . . . He shrugged his shoulders.

His gesture filled her with loneliness. "Please don't leave Antigua without coming to see me." She spoke in Spanish to make sure he understood.

"I promise," he said. "I won't leave without saying goodbye."

NINETEEN

A MONTH LATER RICARDO RETURNED. THIS time he didn't phone to warn her. One afternoon, when she was sitting at the back of the market, almost slumbering in morose drowsiness, his face poked around the corner of her stall.

"¡Ricardo!" Jumping up from the chair where she had been sitting, she seized his wrist without thinking that she had never touched him before. The high-altitude sunlight of the mountains had burned his skin without purging it of its pallor. She felt her grip on his wrist; she relaxed her hold and took a step back. "Sakar, Ricardo. La utz a'wech?"

"Utz matiox, Amparo. Y ret?"

"Life is hard," she said in Spanish. She found herself hoping, with the desperation of an adolescent, that he would notice that she had paid a hairdresser in Antigua to wave her hair. She did not know why she had done this. Esperanza teased her that in her husband's absence she was reverting to girlhood. Amparo had laughed, yet she heard a warning in her sister's voice.

Ricardo stood over her. To her shame, she felt his presence as a man; but he was also an old friend to whom she could speak openly. Glancing down the aisle at the nearby stalls, she waved him into her stall and offered him her spare stool.

"I come to the market every day and hope for tourists," she told him. "I try not to spend money and I thank my god that

I have my house and my children . . . I envy you having the money to make that trip."

He hesitated, as though he had not expected such frankness. "And your husband? Has he found a job in the north? Is he sending you *remesas*?"

She avoided his eyes. "My husband's stay in the United States has not been a success."

"He's still there?"

"Still there. Still living with my brother."

"So he could still become successful."

Shame engulfed her. She looked away.

When she looked up, he was shrugging something off his shoulder. "*Re'n q'o jun ya'l q'iak.* I have a red bag."

She started forward in astonishment and dug her fingers into the red weft. "Ricardo, I made this bag!"

"This is the bag I bought two years ago in Chiapas."

"But you said you'd given it to a friend . . . *un amigo*." She could not bring herself to use the feminine form.

"*Una amiga.* I met this *amiga* in Todos Santos Cuchumatán last week. She gave me back the bag."

"This is one of the bags Don Julio sent to be sold in Mexico . . . " Her voice trailed off at the thought of Ricardo, a married man, a man she respected, meeting an *amiga* in a remote town in the mountains. She should end this conversation; she should not speak to him again. Six months ago, she was sure, this was what she would have done. Now, in spite of herself, she felt deluged by sympathy and a contradictory need to understand how his life worked.

A scuffing noise came from the aisle. Four women in *huipiles* had shuffled close to the stall to listen to them. Fortunately, Doña María was not among them. "He is my client," she told them in Cakchiquel.

They tittered and shuffled away.

"Come on," she said to Ricardo in Spanish. "Let's go talk in the square." They walked down the aisle. "Ever since my husband left, I've been surrounded by women who want to spread ugly gossip . . . Let's show them how little I care what they think!"

She linked arms with him. He seemed startled by the gesture — she was startled herself at what she was doing — yet his initial awkwardness melted as he kept stride with her. She pulled him along, recovering an energy that had been buried deep in her body. She basked in her own strength and determination. The women who had gathered in front of her stall scattered like clucking hens. Arm-in-arm, they walked towards the front door of the market. A girl who was learning how to weave on the *tela de cincha* looked up, and the neighbour who was teaching her laid her hand across the girl's eyes, muttering.

"*Ri äk nusik'in chuwajay!* The hen is clucking in my house!" In Spanish she continued: "She should cluck in her own house before she clucks in mine!"

When they reached the bench in the square, she felt herself burst into rollicking laughter. She hadn't laughed this hard in months. "Ay, *mi Dios* . . . Ixmucane is laughing with me . . . I can feel her . . . "

"But, Amparo, your community . . . If they see you walking with a gringo man . . . Won't they . . . ?"

She was laughing too hard to reply. At last she sat up, feeling the tears that glistened on her cheeks. "It used to be like that, Ricardo . . . Even recently. But not any more. This community no longer has the power to destroy anyone's life. It is too weak and unsure of itself. My friend Raquel has done scandalous things — things that are wrong and which I would never do," she added to head off any misunderstanding, "and she continues to live in her house and nothing has happened to her." Watching him absorbing this information, she changed the subject. "There are still just enough tourists coming to the market to keep us all alive. The members of my savings club have suspended their monthly payments. For the moment, we're not giving anyone micro-credit."

"There's no work at Escuela Tecún Umán?"

She shook her head. "A few tourists. No university groups, no missionaries, no State Department. Since the gringos started fighting in Iraq they have stopped coming to Guatemala."

They talked about a Mayan mayor who was running for president, about the latest scandals in the FDR Party. Ricardo looked uncomfortable: "Amparo, the company I work for has collapsed." She regarded him in incomprehension. "It's gone bankrupt. I'm unemployed."

"Do such things happen in your country?"

"Sometimes. Some of the Canadian students may come back next year, but if they do, their universities will arrange it by themselves. I have to go home and look for another job."

"Can't you find a job here?" She was taken aback by the urgency in her voice.

"It's easier if I look at home. At home it's easier for me to see my wife."

"You're lucky that you can see your wife sometimes," Amparo said, her fingers closing around a fold of her *uq*. She was glad that she was wearing this black skirt, whose traditionalism cancelled out the allure of her waved hair.

"I want you to have the bag," he said. When she hesitated, he said: "It's yours. You made it."

He offered it to her. She took the bag in her hands. She was aware of their awkward postures, turned half towards each other on the bench in the deserted square. She looked at his concerned, sunburned face. "You're trying to give me back the culture that's been taken from me," she whispered. "I'm not sure anyone can do that anymore."

"Only you . . . " He shrugged his shoulders. "I don't have any answers. Not for you or me or anybody. But I think you should have the bag."

"Thank you, Ricardo." She realized she would not see him again. He was the last in her line of wealthy, cultured mentors. Don Julio, Sister Consuelo, the señora gringa . . . She would not befriend anyone like this again. Even if she met such people in the future, she was too old to be a *protegida*, a young indigenous woman full of potential. With the fading of post-war optimism, few people cared if Mayan women had potential. She longed to hold onto some shard of those years when her life, her village, her country, had felt as if they could change and grow. On impulse, she asked: "Will your cellphone work in Canada?"

"My cellphone? I bought it here. I assume it won't work in Canada."

"Will you give it to me?"

"Of course." He seemed disappointed. He reached into his pocket and hefted the cellphone in his hand. He leaned forward. "You press that button to — "

"I know how they work."

He did not reply. Up the street a schoolbus honked its intention to leave for Antigua. He got to his feet. "Goodbye, Amparo," he said in a slow voice that came from low in his throat. "I'm very grateful for your friendship."

She stared at him, feeling a longing she could not define. "You will always be my friend."

They shook hands with a slow clasp. She turned away and walked into the market.

PART THREE

2005

TWENTY

WHEN A WOMAN'S HUSBAND HAS left her alone for almost three years, she loses the ability to share. Working away from home like a father, Amparo felt herself to be less of a mother. Even as she promised herself that everything she did was for her family, she worried she was doing less for her children, her parents, her community. Don Teófilo phoned her when missionary groups came to Antigua to learn Spanish, or when a gringo student or professor asked for a Cakchiquel course. But she had no time for Escuela Tecún Umán. For months now she had been on the move, travelling all the time; she would not commit herself to a schedule of going to Antigua every morning.

In the last meeting of the Cakchiquel Women's Savings Club prior to the December 2003 elections, she had urged the young girls to vote. They looked at her with helpless expressions. Their husbands had gone north: like her, they were alone with their children. "You must participate in this society," she told them, "or it will never get better, and your children will leave as well."

"I don't know who to vote for," one of the girls said.

"You don't know that we must get rid of this corrupt FDR government?" Amparo almost lost her temper. "You don't know that? Isn't it obvious?"

Against her own principles, she told them that she would be voting for Óscar Berger, the rich Belgian coffee-grower with the big moustache. Neither a former *militar* nor a former guerrilla, Berger was untainted by the civil war.

She never learned whether the girls had voted, but it was clear that others thought as she did because Berger was elected president. In the village, though, the FDR mayor was re-elected. In the first week of 2004, one of the three civil servants who worked in the town hall next to the market banged on the door of the compound, demanded to see Amparo and handed her an envelope containing a legal document. She leafed through the pages in confusion until she realized that her licence to run a stall had been revoked. The reason given was "commercial malpractice." She had twenty-four hours in which to remove her belongings from the market or they would be impounded by the municipality. The twenty-four-hour period had started twenty-three hours ago.

When she got to the market, police were strolling the aisles. Doña Rosa was sobbing as her daughter helped her stuff her exquisite blankets into plastic bags. *"Anchi jat jech'ël?"* she said when she saw Amparo. "They don't believe I didn't vote . . . How can I vote when I can't read?"

"You've destroyed her life with your stupid club," Doña Rosa's daughter said in Spanish. "You'd better give her back her money. She's going to need it now!"

Doña Soledad, coming in from piling her weavings on a bench in the park, scowled at Amparo. Doña María and her daughter were also packing up their merchandise: they were moving into the stall at the front of the market from which Doña Rosa had been expelled.

"I knew you were using your stall to hide the money you stole from that savings club," Doña María said in a loud voice. "Your corruption . . . !"

"The corrupt person in this village is our mayor!" Amparo shouted.

The police stepped forward. "You're defaming a public official," the older officer said. "You're committing a crime, señora."

"Your mother committed a crime when she gave birth to you!"

The police seized her arms. They were small men, barely taller than she. Their shortness frightened her, reminding her of the Mayan men, press-ganged into the army during the civil war, who had massacred villages full of people like themselves. Their boots scuffed the concrete as they hustled her towards the door. The clear daylight made it even more horrifying that this was happening. She recoiled against them, falling back on her heels. They whipped her forward, shouting that she was a *puta*.

She realized they were going to lock her in the cells in the town hall.

"Save me!" she screamed. "Soledad! Doña Rosa! Don't let them do this to me!" She twisted around, seeking out her companions from the Cakchiquel Women's Savings Club. Humble women bent over plastic bags. The young girls stood with their arms around each other's shoulders, pretending not to watch what was happening to her. "Tell Esperanza," she gasped, as the men hustled her across the stone. "Tell my sister — "

Their fingers slipped on the snarled sleeve of her blouse. The door of the town hall appeared in front of them. She dug her heels in. "No!" she said. "I've done nothing wrong. You're supposed to enforce the law — "

"¡*Puta!*" the younger one said, punching her in the shoulder as she half-succeeded in wriggling free. This boy's youngest sister used to play with Sandra.

"How's your little sister?" she asked, reeling from the ache spreading through her shoulder. She retreated from the door of the town hall in slow backward steps.

They crept towards her. The older policeman glanced at the younger one. She kept moving backwards, sensing women spying on them from the door of the market.

The men halted, their crouched combat postures stiffening. Amparo realized they were looking over her shoulder. She glanced around and saw Raquel approaching. She wore a black Mayan skirt with a black Western blouse; her hair was loose.

"Let her go," Raquel said. "She's done nothing wrong."

The police slipped into the apologetic slouch of poor men. "She defamed the mayor," the older policeman said, shrugging his shoulders.

"If you don't let her go, you'll regret it."

Raquel was the *curandera*. In spite of their uniforms, these men feared the spells she could cast on their families.

"My gringo friend is coming on Saturday," Raquel said. "When he complains to the United States Ambassador, you'll be the ones who go to jail."

"We're not doing anything against the United States," the older man said.

"We're not doing anything against the Ambassador," the younger man said.

"Then let her go," Raquel said.

The policemen shrugged their shoulders and walked towards the town hall.

Raquel gave Amparo a hug. Amparo resisted for an instant, then felt herself bite back on sobs as she crumpled into Raquel's arms. "Go clear out your stall before they steal your weaving," Raquel said. "Then come and see me."

When she returned to the market, no one spoke. The women from her club avoided her; the Evangelicals and the Catholics did not speak to each other; the women who had returned to Mayan spirituality gave both groups the cold shoulder. A vast sadness clogged her at the sight of the village's women separating their belongings into antagonistic clusters. At last, she lugged her textiles towards the door. She was despairing of carrying them home, along with her loom, stools, wooden poles and coathangers, when Esperanza arrived. Taking turns, they carried everything back to the compound and piled it in Amparo's living room. Amparo hugged her sister and went to see Raquel.

Through the flaking paint on the front door, she heard the baby crying. Raquel stepped forward with the child in her arms. "I'm sorry I couldn't help you move your weaving. I can't leave her alone . . . "

Amparo kissed Raquel's mud-brown long-armed daughter on the forehead. "She's so big. And barely a month old!" As Raquel ushered her inside, she said: "Is he really coming to see you?"

"Yes," Raquel said. "I'm able to see my lover, unlike all the women who never see their husbands. If I hadn't acted on my fantasies, I'd still be waiting for Jorge to come home."

"Is that all you want to tell me?" Amparo said. "After I've lost everything?"

Raquel brushed Amparo's sleeve with a cursory caress, as though maternity had rendered her brusque. "The world we fought for is gone. You've always had a mixture of cultures, Amparo — like my daughter. Don't be afraid to let who you are guide your life."

Too upset to continue the conversation, Amparo left. The next week she turned over the job of chairing the Cakchiquel Women's Savings Club to Esperanza. She went to Antigua and scoured the spots where Mayan women who lacked licences used to sell their weaving to tourists: the courtyard of a ruined cathedral that was open to the public, a small park a few blocks from the centre, the entrances of various tourist attractions. In every case, the informal mini-markets had been closed; white-armbanded tourist police walked their beats to ensure that the selling of textiles was limited to souvenir shops and licensed stalls. She went to see Don Teófilo, but he could offer her only odd hours with individual tourists. The Canadians and their little Chinese professor had not come back this year. "And Don Ricardo?" Amparo asked, keeping her voice steady.

"When I asked, I was told he's no longer in Canada."

He had moved to another country, like Sister Consuelo and the señora gringa. He was immersed in someone else's problems. All these people had cared about her country, but their care was spread too thinly over the surface of the world. Only she could look after herself. Her responsibilities stood before her mind's eye: Sandra and Pablito, Mama and Papa, her debt to Yoli and David, her duty to Eusebio. They appeared to her as chores on a list, all of secondary importance to the throbbing reality of her senses, her abilities that craved an outlet, her determination to thrive. She felt as crushed by the news that the Canadians were not returning as by the loss of her stall. She had got used to those quieter gringos who wanted to make the world better even though they did not talk about God. The Canadians' arrival in Antigua every January had become her life, just as volcanoes and June rains and God and Ixmucane were her life. Her existence was slipping away from her, driving all of her habits, even Eusebio — the Eusebio she had loved, not the hectic voice on the phone — deeper into the past.

The next time he called she warned him that next Sunday she might be away. He went quiet. She reminded him that she had no income. He became furious. She didn't realize how hard it was for him to save money! After being fired from his job bagging groceries — he never explained why — he had been unemployed for weeks. Now he was cleaning windshields at a gas station. "I have to feed the children," she said, "I have to pay for Sandra's *colegio*, I have to pay back the money we owe Yoli for your *coyote*. I give her money whenever I can, but we still owe them more than thirty-eight thousand quetzales. You don't — "

He hung up.

TWENTY-ONE

I N ESCUINTLA, A FILTHY *LADINO* city near the Pacific Coast, she could sell her weaving without paying a licence fee. She met other Mayan women who were doing as she was, extending Mayanness to the least aboriginal corners of *Ixim Ulew.* At the end of the day five or six of them would share a room in the cheapest hotel behind the market. Before falling asleep on the floor on her weavings, she called home on Ricardo's cellphone. She made sure that Sandra had cooked supper for her brother and helped him with his homework. Her stomach twisted at the thought of how Pablito was struggling at the terrible village school. Sandra did her best to help him, but she spent much of the evening cooking and cleaning. More and more, she looked after the house on her own. Mama had gone over to help her at first; now, when Amparo returned to the compound, her mother praised her daughter's maturity. *"Ri ixtën roto' ri rute'.* The señorita helps her mother. She puts her little brother to bed like a second mother." Mama's words followed her on long bus trips, making her feel guilty each time she reprimanded Sandra for her adolescent boldness.

When Mama wasn't there, Sandra was alone with Pablito. Soon after Amparo lost her stall in the market, Inés, overcoming her fear of men, ran away with one of the clerks at the hotel. They disappeared from Antigua; it was as if the girl had never passed through her life.

The next summer, on a rainy day in Escuintla, the man at the stall next to hers invited her to crouch beneath the tarpaulin he had strung over a wooden frame to protect the stainless steel pots he was selling. As they watched the rain pounding the market's aisles to mud, he told her that she was a very beautiful woman. A bolt of terror shot through her. If it hadn't been for the rain she would have left. She looked at him with care. He was a *ladino* in his late thirties, broader shouldered and lighter skinned than other men she knew, with narrow features and the trace of a moustache. "Has your husband gone north?" In spite of the unwelcomeness of this question, she felt sympathy beneath his words. "Does he have a woman there? Children?"

"My husband doesn't have another woman," she said.

"How do you know?"

She shrugged her shoulders, feeling a chill in her stomach at the thought of how far away her Eusebio had gone. She stayed there next to Pedro. They spoke all day, the rain having driven away their customers. He told her that he had grown up in his father's hardware store. Then his father had begun to drink; they had lost the store. "Now, you can always find me here, selling in the market." In the evening she dropped her wares in her hotel room, then went with him to a bar where she drank the first Gallo beer of her life. It tasted like dark river-water swimming with pyrites. Her head turned light and her thighs felt heavy; Pedro's moustache took on an enticing curve. On the television over the bar, the host said: *"To discuss the day's political events, we have our regular commentator, Edmundo Rodríguez . . . "*

Comandante Vladimir. Though he no longer used that name, she would always remember the thrill of possibility, of the world opening wider to accommodate ways of thinking other than the military way, that had gripped her the first time she had seen him on the small screen. Watching him now, heavier in the jowls, his moustache greying, she imagined she saw a calculation in his eyes that had not been there when he had appeared as the spokesman for the *guerrilla*. "The Peace Accords were good to people like him," she coughed, "just not to the rest of us."

A wash of her youthful energy revived as Pedro responded to her with a smile and drained his second Gallo. He told her about his business, raised his hand to order a third beer, then, as she stared at him, waved the waiter away. "That's enough for one evening," he said with a smile whose softness made her head reel. She told him how the mayor had taken away her licence. He grasped the horror of this experience as no one else had. He walked her back to her hotel. As he took her hand, she felt herself completing the closeness of their conversation. When he led her into a gap between two houses, she felt the heat of his beery mouth on hers like a consolation. The warmth of his hands on her hips stirred her womb into a fury. She sought the bulk of his body, grappling against him with a sob. Three years! She started to kiss him as hard as he was kissing her. She was trussed up in his heat when shrieks erupted next to her ears. Two teenage girls, stopped on the sidewalk, were laughing at them. The younger one looked like Sandra.

"We're covered in mud," she said, holding him back. She glanced down at her spattered black skirt. As she stepped out from beneath the overhang between the houses, rain washed her face without cleansing it.

He gripped her elbow. "Come with me. I have a room — "

"I'm a married woman — " She didn't go on, determined that he not see her in tears.

In the doorway of her hotel she allowed him to kiss her, aware of the kiss as a farewell. Her enjoyment of his mouth appalled her. It didn't matter what Eusebio had done over the last three years, she was his wife. She went to the room where the other women were asleep, and lay down on her bundled weaving. Her damp skirt made her teeth chatter. She felt revolted. She was a señora. Imagine the shame if she got pregnant again. At her age! It wouldn't have been like Raquel and her gringo. She would have tipped Sandra and Pablito deeper into poverty by adding another mouth to feed. Pedro . . . A man whose name she had learned only a few hours ago. She had never allowed Ezequial to do more than hold her hand and put his arm around her waist . . . During the five years when Eusebio had been her *novio* she had never pressed her body against his with such voraciousness . . . She had been young then, a virgin whose body lacked a wife's knowledge; now she was a wife with married knowledge and shameful needs that had no outlet.

When the other women turned on the light at four thirty, she groaned with a headache. They laughed at her. She brushed dried mud off her skirt and pulled together her wares. She followed the others to the market in the dark, then slipped away to the yard where the buses waited. She travelled in silence, looking out the window at the world God had made. The thought that she had repaid Him for His bounty by staining her marriage refused to leave her head. The sickness was as unforgiving as her headache, which throbbed harder as the cloudy morning broke around the flanks of the volcanoes. Fumes from the bus' leaky exhaust drenched the back seats. Her fall from grace had sprung from a self-centredness that was the result of having been left alone for three years. Even as she clenched her teeth, insisting that Eusebio was to blame, she knew that she must take responsibility. She prayed in the rattling seat of the bus. In matters of sin she always prayed to God; Ixmucane and Xpiyacoc responded to her longings, her need to defend her family, her quest to fit herself into the arc of the world. Now Hurricane peeped down at her from the heart of the sky. *Your life will be full of dangers, the path forward is not clear and may not be lengthy. You will endure these trials only if you have help from your family.* Her path was her own, that of the jaguars she wove into her red bags. The jaguar was her *nahual*, though she could divulge this to no one. Only Doña Manuela had perceived this identity.

If she died, all that would matter would be the life she bequeathed to her children. Her family had lifted itself through hard work from poverty to a level of basic security, even moderate prosperity; but advancement through hard work was no longer possible. The families that were advancing now had fathers who earned dollars in the north, or brothers who ran drugs for the *maras*.

If only Eusebio would send his *remesas* like other men!

And if he didn't send them? What was the best security she could give her children?

For the next week she was restless and unable to sleep. When she turned on the light at night, the photographs on the mantle stared back at her: her wedding, her late mother-in-law. The bag Ricardo had returned to her hung from a peg. She got up in the morning to make breakfast for her children and wove at her loom in the living room all day as rain fell in the compound outside. She made tourist waistcoats, bags woven in dayglo colours that said *Souvenir of Guatemala*. In the evening she supervised Sandra and Pablito's homework. Her mother was right about Sandra: she was outgoing and competent. She was like her mother and delighted in arranging facts into categories. Poor Pablito was lost. He was eight years old and could barely read or write.

Something must change. She ransacked her mind, trying to think of all the ways in which she could improve her children's lives.

Next morning, after the children left for school, she made a phone call. "Yoli," she said, "how much money do I owe you?"

"Thirty-seven thousand six hundred and fifty quetzales. I know it's not your fault that Eusebio doesn't send *remesas*, Amparo, but it's embarrassing — "

"Would you lend me more money?"

"What? Amparo — "

"I want to send the children north. Will you help me?"

"Amparo, we've already lent you forty thousand! . . . Why do you want to get rid of your children? What kind of mother are you?"

"They have no future here. They'll have to go north when they grow up. It's better to send them when they're young. They'll learn English and go to school — "

"I can't believe you're saying this! You wouldn't . . . if your husband were here . . . "

"That's another reason. If Eusebio has the children, he'll remember that he's their father and support them. He'll work harder and you'll get paid back sooner."

"It's monstrous! Don't you love your children, Amparo?"

"Yes, that's why I'm doing this. I could be selfish and hold onto my children twice as tightly because my husband has left. Love is thinking of what's good for the other person." She stopped, realizing she had been about to make the mistake of telling Yoli that she would understand if she had children.

"Have you talked to Eusebio about this?"

"Not yet." Amparo felt her sister's embarrassed silence. She drew a breath to steady herself. "I know what you think. You think he has another woman there. Well maybe he does, I don't know. If Rafael knows anything, he doesn't tell me. But Eusebio's still my husband. He'll see his responsibilities the first time his children smile at him."

It was hopeless. She sat down at the table, but it wasn't enough to prevent the sobs from weakening her grasp on the receiver.

"Yoli . . . "

"Get a glass of water, Amparo, then come back to the phone. I'm thinking."

She put down the receiver, wondering when this insouciant little girl had started to give her orders. She wiped her cheeks, sipped a glass of water, and sat down beneath the tattoo of rain on the corrugated roof.

As she sipped, she thought about her decision. She must be twisted. What kind of mother wanted to be separated from her children? She was the worst woman on earth. Yet she could not get the plan out of her head. Some deep urge was driving her to send the children away. She took another sip of water and picked up the receiver again.

"Amparo," Yoli said. "I promise I'll help. I don't know exactly how or how much, but I'll find money or get David to find some."

"He won't be angry?"

"Right now," Yoli said, "David owes me a few favours."

Amparo held the receiver in silence, wondering whether her sister wished to say more about this. "Thank you," she said.

"I won't be able to pay it all, Amparo. Everybody in the family will have to contribute. You need to find out how much this is going to cost. And are you sure they'll be safe? How can you trust your children to a *coyote*?"

After their conversation ended, she sat in silence and listened to the rain on the roof. Finding out how much it was going to cost would make the act real. It would mean that her children were leaving.

She got to her feet and walked into the bedroom. Her attention settled on the jaguar prowling across the red weft. On a scrap of paper in a drawer she found the cellphone number of Eusebio's *coyote*. Would the number still work? She walked into the living room and lifted the receiver.

"*Aló,*" a curt voice said, beset by static.

"My name is Amparo Ajuix. You helped my husband, Eusebio Hernández." She waited to see whether this was the right number.

"And?"

"I want to send two children on a trip. How much would it cost?"

"What ages?"

"Eight and twelve. I want the trip to be very smooth. I don't want them to suffer."

"One hundred thousand."

"So much?"

"If you want the best service. Children cost more."

"I'll call you when I have the money."

It was too much. The plan could wait till next year. But when the children came home, she was reminded that Sandra's breasts had grown more defined. In a few months she would face the same danger of being raped as all women who travelled north.

You will endure these trials only if you have help from your family. That night, after putting the children to bed, she went to see Mama and Papa. They sat around their gas stove as though it were an open fireplace. Papa sucked on his cigarette while Mama, with two buckets at her feet, separated beans from chaff. "*Ri nu akua'l,*" Mama said when she came in the door. "My child." She saw that her mother was alert to the seriousness of her manner. As Amparo faltered, Mama said: "If you wish to join your husband, we can look after your children."

"No," she said. "I want you to help me send the children to live with my husband."

"You're a mother, my daughter," her father said. "Your children — "

He looked to his wife for support. Mama looked at the floor. After a long silence, she said: "My grandchildren will have better lives." She paused. "My great-grandchildren will be gringos."

"Mama, they'll still — "

"My great-grandchildren will be gringos." She shook her head, then laid her hand on Amparo's arm. "*Ja. Utz.* We'll help."

The next week Papa put up for sale the fringe of land that ran around the outside of the compound, where he had planned to grow potatoes in his retirement. As soon as he went to the town hall to register the sale, the mayor made an offer on the plot.

"Papa," Amparo said. "Don't sell to our enemy."

"He's the mayor. If I don't sell to him, he won't let me sell to anyone else."

Between Yoli's money, which had come from David, and Papa's money, which had come from the mayor, Amparo had nearly a hundred thousand quetzales. Esperanza offered a slice of her tiny savings, as did her brother Fernando and his wife. Amparo accepted each contribution in silence. She thanked God for giving her such a generous family. She rolled the money into the rabbit god blanket and hid it in Inés' room. She paced the tiles. Finally, taking out Ricardo's cellphone, she called the number.

201

"This is Amparo Ajuix," she said. "To send two children north . . . I have the money."

She heard the drone of an engine. "Tomorrow," the voice said at last. Then he said: "They can leave tomorrow."

"Tomorrow?"

"Yes. I have two spaces."

"All right," she gasped. "Tomorrow."

"At one o'clock in the afternoon. One hundred thousand in cash."

"Come at three," she said. "They'll be back from school."

A puzzled silence. She imagined the man wondering why a final day of school could matter. He agreed to the time. She hung up, ran to her bedroom, and cried on her bed with long, inconsolable gasps that were like giving birth in reverse.

She got up, went to the children's bedroom, and weighed in her hands the infant toys in which they were losing interest. She washed her face in the bathroom. Her heart continued to flutter. Digging an umbrella out of the corner, she walked out of the house and the compound. When she reached the square, she knocked on Raquel's door.

Raquel answered with her daughter at her ankles. Now that the girl was eighteen months old, her features had taken on a blunt, oblong quality. She had tanned skin, wispy brown hair, Willard J. Franklin's tray-like jaw and little of Raquel's enticing delicacy. Dressed in a red corduroy jump suit, the girl greeted Amparo with a loud bleat of greeting that sounded as though she were trying to say, "*Sakar!*"

"I need to talk," Amparo whispered.

"I'm about to put her down for her nap," Raquel said.

Amparo watched the girl parade across the floor on her long legs. She wondered whether her grandchildren would look like

Raquel's daughter. Miserable guilt clawed at her. She sat down in a chair.

When Raquel returned fifteen minutes later, easing the door shut behind her, she gave her a hug. "What's the matter?"

"Tomorrow," Amparo said, "I'm sending away my children."

"What do you mean?"

As Amparo explained, she remembered the village where they had met: the Evangelical girl who spoke Spanish and the Catholic girl who spoke Cakchiquel. For all their differences, they had never doubted that they would bring up their children together around this dusty park.

Raquel shook her head. "I could never send her away."

"You should think about it. Do you think your gringo will let his daughter go to school here?"

"He wants her to speak Cakchiquel." Raquel made one objection after another to Amparo's plans, their conversation weaving between Cakchiquel and Spanish. "Pablo needs his culture. He has real potential as a daykeeper. If he leaves . . . "

"He's a weak boy, Raquel. Life is hard here. He'll be better off . . . "

"And what are you going to do after your children are gone?"

"Earn my living and promote my culture," she said. "I'll sell my weaving. If the mayor's defeated in the next election, I might get my stall back."

"You won't be here then. You do realize that, Amparo? You won't be able to stand being separated from your children."

She herself in the north? She shook her head.

"You don't realize how lonely you're going to feel." Raquel leaned forward. "Don't leave, Amparo," she whispered. "I won't be able to stand it!" She faltered. "When I left the Evangelicals . . . you have no idea how important your example was to me. You're vital to those girls in your club . . . You don't see the role you play in keeping our culture alive here. *Tab'ana utzil, tab'ana utzil* . . . I beg you, I beg you . . . I know it's horrible when a husband leaves . . . *Re'n ninna utz lo ke ret xa q'ax* . . . I'm very sorry about what happened to you. But don't leave."

"I'll never leave, Raquel."

"You will if you send your children away! But when you go, you won't travel like them! Your family is out of money, your father's getting too old to work as a *piloto*. The rest of you are poor. You'll have to travel with a cheap *coyote*. You'll be locked in the back of a truck and raped by the Mexican police and jailed by the gringos. Don't do this, Amparo."

Amparo stared at the Mayan calendar on the wall. "Our culture tells us that the world has been created and destroyed many times. We live in the future only through our children."

"And your husband? If your children go north and your husband looks after them, won't you want to resume your marriage?"

"By sending him the children, I'm showing him we're no less married because we live in different countries."

"You don't have a man here? You're not getting rid of your children to be with your lover?"

"Raquel! I'm not like that!" Not like you, she almost said. She saw Raquel's thin features tighten. She got to her feet. "Your daughter will wake up soon."

"Think carefully before you do this, Amparo."

"I'm thinking . . . ! *Xaj.*"

She tried to make the evening perfect. She barely responded when, after supper, Sandra reeled off the names of the good secondary schools her classmates would be attending. "Señora Machojón says I could go to one of those schools, too, but she doesn't know if my parents have enough money."

"I don't know if we have enough money either," she said in a mild voice, determined not to let Sandra lure her into a fight. She hugged and squeezed her. The girl was almost as tall as she; the hardness of her immature breasts made Amparo feel that her own body was becoming soft. Pablito ran over and battered his hands against their hips. "Let me hug you, too!" Amparo embraced her children; she drew a long breath. Then Sandra pulled away, ordering Pablito to help her wash the dishes.

When they went to bed, she thought about phoning Eusebio. But she still wasn't sure. If she decided to go ahead with this, she would send the children to Rafael's house.

In the morning, she listened to the rain on the roof. She cooked Sandra and Pablito a breakfast of fried eggs and toast. "Just like the gringos!" Sandra said, as she brought the plates to the table.

Amparo turned away.

When the children had left for school, she packed their bags, choosing the essentials: underwear, T-shirts, bluejeans, a jacket each against the cold northern nights. As three o'clock approached, she carried the bags out of the bedroom and dropped them on the couch. She walked across the deserted compound to wait for the knock on the gate. When it came, the *coyote* slouched in, the heel of his right foot dragging soft slurs in the mud. They walked in silence to the house. She made him wipe his feet before he came in. She invited him to sit on the living room couch next to the children's travel bags and went to Inés' room for the money.

"One hundred thousand," he said, when he had counted the money. "When will the children be here?"

"Any moment now. Can I ask you, señor, how my children will arrive at the appropriate place?"

"It's better if you don't know."

"I don't want them to suffer!"

"They won't suffer. They'll cross the border in a car with documents that show them to be the children of a wealthy Chicano family."

He smiled at his lapse. Her glance plunged to his right foot, which splayed outward like a fawn's cleft hoof. "What did you do before you were a *coyote?*" When he didn't reply, she said: "We've met before."

"When I came for your husband," he said.

"Not only then."

His eyes opened to a wideness brimming with hostility. She should never give her children to this man.

He counted his money and put it in his pocket.

The murmur of voices, the rattle of the doorhandle, and Sandra burst in, waving her schoolbag. At the sight of the stranger she fell silent. She circled the couch, sidled up to Amparo's chair, and stared at the man again. Pressing her lips against Amparo's ear, she whispered in a breath of hot air: *"Mama, is that your boyfriend?"*

Amparo seized Sandra's wrist and hustled her into her bedroom. She closed the door and, in the same swing of her arm, slapped her daughter across the cheek. Sandra looked too stunned to cry. Amparo gripped her wrists. "I want you to remember something for the rest of your life: marriage is forever! It doesn't matter how far away she is, a woman is always loyal to her husband. That's what it's like for Papa and me. And that's what it will be like for you when you're grown up."

"But Raquel — "

"Raquel is a bad example."

"But she's your *friend!*" Sandra said.

Her daughter needed her; she couldn't trust her upbringing to chance. She hugged Sandra. The girl began to sob. Amparo spent so long comforting her that she wondered whether the *coyote* would still be there when they returned to the front room.

She opened the door to find Pablito sitting on the couch. "Mama!" he said. "This man's taking me to see Papa!"

The *coyote* looked down at his tiny hands with a smile that stoked her confidence in him.

Sandra turned on her. "Pablito's going to see Papa and I'm not?"

She glanced in the direction of the *coyote*, wondering whether he would give her back half the money.

"I want to go, too," Sandra said.

"All right," Amparo said. "But you must promise me that you will always remember what I just told you."

"I promise, Mama."

Amparo waved at the bags on the couch. "Go and change out of your school clothes."

They whooped, ran into the bedroom, and changed in record speed. Their enthusiasm raked her with pain; she remembered Eusebio's wisdom in refusing to say goodbye to his children.

Pablito returned first. He fumbled with the zipper of his travel bag.

"Don't worry," Amparo said, leaning forward. "Everything you need is in there."

"Can I take the jaguar?"

"The jaguar?" For a moment she didn't know what he meant. She went to her bedroom and lifted the bag off the hook. She rubbed her fingertips over the bunched threads. Returning to the front room, she displayed the bag; Pablito nodded in satisfaction. She unzipped his satchel and slipped the bag inside. Pablito smiled. "*B'alam.*" He took a breath. "*Re'n jin Pablo*," he said. "I am Pablo."

The *coyote* was pacing. Her children hugged her as though they were leaving for the afternoon. Her heart burned in her chest. She told herself they must not see her misery. As they walked down the path on either side of the *coyote*, she thought: I've given my children to a criminal.

She closed the door and watched them out the window. Across the sodden blossoms of the bougainvillea, she saw the *coyote* open the metal gate and wave the children forward. Sandra and Pablito left the compound without looking back. Dragging his maimed foot, the *coyote* closed the gate.

Her fingers clutched. She would have to work hard to pay back her debt. This evening she would phone Rafael, then she would bundle up her weaving. At five o'clock tomorrow morning she would go to Antigua, where she would change to the bus that would take her to Guatemala City, and from there to the market in Escuintla.

She stared out the window until she was certain it was too late to run and pull her children out of the car.

ACKNOWLEDGEMENTS

Among the many Guatemalans and Canadians working in Guatemala who have contributed to my eternally unfinished apprenticeship in the country's culture, I would like to thank Anabella Acevedo Leal, Kurt Annen, Margarita Asensio, Kalowatie Deonandan, Candace Johnson, Kris Inwood, Lisa Maldonado, Carlos Mendoza, Arturo Miranda, Lilia Pérez Marín, Tomás Rosada, Julio Serrano, and James Sim.

I am very grateful to Al Forrie and Jackie Forrie at Thistledown Press for their support over many years. I am also enormously grateful to my editor, Seán Virgo, who improved my prose here, as in four earlier books, with an insight and perception that I wish I had myself.

A section of this novel originally appeared in *Numéro Cinq*.

STEPHEN HENIGHAN is the author of three previous novels, including *The Streets of Winter*. His short stories have been published in more than 40 magazines and anthologies on both sides of the Atlantic. A columnist for *Geist*, Henighan has published articles and reviews in *The Times Literary Supplement*, *Toronto Life*, *The Walrus*, *Guernica*, *The Quarterly Conversation*, *The Globe and Mail*, the *Montreal Gazette*, and *The Literary Review of Canada*. He has translated novels into English from Portuguese and Romanian; books by him have been published in German and Romanian translation. He has been a finalist for, among other prizes, the Governor General's Literary Award, the Canada Prize in the Humanities, a National Magazine Award, a Western Magazine Award, a McNally Robinson Fiction Prize, and the Malahat Novella Prize.

Stephen Henighan teaches Spanish American literature and culture in the Hispanic Studies section of the School of Languages and Literatures at the University of Guelph.